THE ISLAND THIEF

THE ISLAND THIEF

Joe Robbins Book Four

PATRICK KELLY

Dear Wileys,

Enjoy The trip, and say
hello to Selene for me.

Patt

CHAPARRAL PRESS, LLC.

BOOKS BY PATRICK KELLY

In the Joe Robbins Series

The Entrepreneurs

The Cartel Banker

A Siren's Love

The Island Thief

Other Crime Novels

Only Yes Means Yes

Chapter 1

ON THE MORNING I took the ferry to Santorini, the sky was overcast, a rare weather occurrence for Athens in the summer. The overnight rain had washed away the dust and turned the streets dark and shiny and clean.

I stowed my bag in the cargo area and climbed up to the passenger deck to have a look around. The ship had a capacity for five hundred, with two levels for parking and cargo and a third for passengers. There were café bars at either end with assigned seating in between. The aft bar was not crowded, so I ordered a coffee and peered down through the window to the loading area.

My phone said 7:30 a.m., five minutes before departure. The passengers had finished boarding, and the crew was making ready to retrieve the gangplank when a dark sedan with an Uber sign in the windshield pulled to a quick stop on the road fifty yards away. Two American backpackers scrambled to get their gear from the trunk. Without checking to see if his companion was ready, the young man ran for the ship. He had closely cropped black hair and a dark complexion. The young woman struggled to get her arms through the straps and lift her carry bag. But she was in good shape, and once she had everything sorted, she ran at full tilt carrying fifty pounds of gear. Seconds after she came aboard, the crew cast off.

I finished my coffee and walked to my assigned seat to read the *Financial Times*. I had plenty of time to kill, for the trip would take seven hours. I read the paper, took a nap, and then picked up a novel. Occasionally, I glanced out the window.

The opaque brownish water near the port had given way to the dark blue of the sea. The sun broke through the clouds and brightened the water. Fishing boats bobbed lazily nearby, and we passed a small rocky island. Passengers around me began to stir awake and mosey to the bar for snacks and drinks.

I opted to go to the upper deck for some air, and on the way, I walked by the American backpackers in their seats. He read from a dog-eared paperback and she slept, leaning on his shoulder. They appeared to be in their mid-twenties, graduate students perhaps, a little more than a decade older than my girls.

On the topside deck, a salt-scented breeze cooled my face. The crowd was young and split between Greeks and foreigners, mostly American. I made out accents from various parts of the US—the Northeast, California, even a few from Texas. Some of them smoked cigarettes. One kid passed a bottle of vodka around to his friends. I went below for a leisurely lunch and then returned to the upper deck to watch us make two intermediate stops at other islands in the Aegean.

At two thirty, a larger island came into view on the horizon—Santorini—my home for the next six weeks.

Rose had taken Chandler and Callie to Breckenridge, Colorado, to stay at the second home she and her husband Dave had bought. To Rose's credit, she had asked me if it was okay to take the kids for that long. I would miss them, but at the same time, how could I rightly keep the girls from enjoying the fruits of

Rose and Dave's labor? Everyone dreamed of escaping Austin's relentless heat during July and August.

The idea for the Santorini trip had come from a woman I dated a while ago—Alyssa Stavros—a nice Greek girl, now engaged to a nice Greek boy.

"Hey," Alyssa had said, "you should talk to my Uncle Giorgos. He owns a hotel in Santorini, and I think he could use your help."

Giorgos Papadopoulos—whom I had video-conferenced with several times—had seen the margins on one of his businesses—a twenty-four-room boutique hotel—decline in the past year, which made no sense given the strong tourist economy. Giorgos told me his hotelier friends were bragging of record profits. He and his bookkeeper were stumped as to the problem, and he offered me a sweet deal on a room to come and analyze his financial results. I could stay for as long as I wanted.

How serendipitous. I booked a flight and packed a bag.

"Beaches, babes, and booze," my thirteen-year-old daughter Chandler had said sarcastically when she heard about my trip.

So far I had enjoyed none of Chandler's first two items and little of the third. After five days of travel and Athens sightseeing, I had booked my ferry trip. Having done some advance research, I knew of the physical contours of the island, but the reality was another experience altogether.

When I first spotted the whitewashed buildings on top of the cliffs, they looked like snowdrifts. So magnificent was the view that I grew dizzy and reached for the handrail.

Santorini was once a round-shaped landmass, but around the year 1600 BC, a volcano blew out the middle. The blast created a plume of smoke and ash that some experts believe engulfed and wiped out the Minoan civilization on Crete forty miles to the south. The mouth of the volcano collapsed to leave a crescent-shaped island with a caldera that filled with crystal blue water twelve hundred feet deep. Along the inside of the crescent, steep cliffs rose a thousand feet from the sea.

During the intervening years, island inhabitants dug cave homes into the cliffs of the caldera. Then, in the early 1900s, industrious Greeks realized they inhabited one of the most spectacular views on Earth, and they began converting cave homes into hotels for the tourist trade.

The ferry motored across the caldera from west to east toward the port of Athiniós. In the center of the caldera, three small islands remained, one of which—Nea Kameni—was an active volcano. To the ship's north, on the inside of the crescent, lay Fira, the largest town on the island and a tourist mecca; cruise ships pulled into the harbor on a daily basis.

My hotel was in the smaller town of Imerovigli, two miles north of Fira. White buildings built on the top and sides of the cliffs stretched in one continuous line from Fira to Imerovigli. Another six miles to the north lay Oia, a hot tourist stop at the far end of the island where an informal celebration of the sunset was held every day. To the south of me, the crescent curved for another five miles, but that section was mostly undeveloped.

I called the hotel to let them know I had arrived. A young man promised to send a driver named Petros and told me where to meet him.

The ferry cruised into port, and I let the other passengers scramble off the observation deck to retrieve their luggage. From the starboard side, I watched the ship nestle up to the dock. The port town was composed of casual restaurants, rental-car storefronts, hotel brokers, and souvenir shops.

The sun now owned the sky, and the air had grown hot. I grabbed my bag and made my way to an outdoor seat at the café the hotel clerk had mentioned. The awning created welcome shade, and I ordered a Diet Coke.

I had just finished when a light brown van from my hotel pulled to a stop nearby. The van bore the hotel's name on its side: Liakáda Suites. According to the Internet, Liakáda meant sunshine.

Petros jumped out. He was short, stocky, about forty, and dressed in clean cotton slacks and a blue polo shirt that sported the hotel's logo. Petros was affable but spoke little English. With signs and gestures, he helped me load my bag into the back of the van and offered me a seat in the row behind him. I chose to ride shotgun.

We drove up switchback turns on the side of the cliff until we reached the top and entered a paved two-lane road that ran south to north on the western side of the island. The road curved through arid terrain filled with rocks, scrub bushes, and a few houses. Occasional signs pointed inland to vineyards that boasted free tastings for tourists.

Petros kept his eyes on the road and drove at a reasonable speed. Local economy-sized sedans rushed past us. He slowed down and then passed several tourists riding rented four-wheelers with low cruising speed. The rocks opened up on the left to reveal a stunning view of the sea.

We came to a stretch of road bordered on the right by a construction fence. The construction site appeared idle even though it was a weekday. On the other side of the fence, a speeding vehicle on a dirt track trailed a ton of dust. The dirt track and car were angled to intersect with our road in a hundred yards. The other vehicle—a black Mercedes—showed no sign of braking to give us the right of way. I glanced at Petros to make sure he had noticed our collision course. He hadn't.

"Watch it," I shouted.

He yelled in Greek and slammed on the brakes.

The Mercedes ran through the intersection into our lane. Our tires squealed, and Petros swerved left. Finally, the Mercedes braked—kicking up rocks and dirt—and spun to a harrowing stop not twenty feet from us.

Petros sat stunned, breathing hard. He shook his head, blinked a few times, and pulled the van onto the shoulder. Then he stepped out to check on the other car. I turned in my seat to watch through the rear window. The other driver—a casually dressed man in his thirties—got out of the Mercedes and began yelling at Petros. Petros stood still with his shoulders hunched and his face upturned. He took the lecture timidly, nodding. He seemed to know the other man.

Heat rose in my chest. My heart thumped from the near collision. I watched the yahoo who almost got us killed bawl out Petros, and the muscles in my arms grew tense. I stepped out of the car to find the air thick with heat and dust. The guy grabbed Petros's shirtfront and slapped him across the face.

The yahoo's body was well proportioned with thick legs, a trim waist, and broad shoulders. He wore his dark hair short. Petros made no move to defend himself, and the man slapped him again.

"Hey!" I said. "Easy. *You're* the one who can't drive."

I strode toward them, and the guy dropped Petros's shirt. An old truck slowed on the road to rubberneck and then kept going.

The bully smiled. He was six feet tall and maybe two hundred pounds. I had a few inches, a few years, and twenty pounds on him, but he must have thought tourists couldn't fight because when he turned toward me, his expression said he intended to give me a few slaps as well.

The rear window of the Mercedes came down, and someone in the back called out, "Can we go now, Markos?" The voice spoke with an English accent.

"Just a minute," said Markos.

"Maybe you'd better go," I said, stopping four feet from him, close enough to communicate that I wasn't afraid but not so close that I would invade his personal space. Petros chattered in Greek, supplicating Markos, but Markos shoved him away.

"I'll leave in a minute," said Markos. He stepped closer to me and telegraphed his next move: a right haymaker punch. I rocked back to let it go by, and he shuffled to keep his balance.

"It's not too late," I said. I edged backward, and the heels of my feet rose a fraction of an inch. Frustrated, Markos threw a second punch with his right, but I dodged that one as well.

He pulled his fists up and awkwardly bounced on his feet. My left fist rose to the front of my face, the right behind it and lower. I threw a left jab that clipped his forehead. His head snapped back.

"Last chance," I said.

He tried a wild punch with his left. I let it go by and threw a straight right to his body, a lot of power behind the punch. He grunted, doubled over, and struggled to breathe.

I backed away but kept my fists ready, not sure whether he was done. My breathing was easy, my heart rate steady.

"Markos," insisted the voice from the back of the Mercedes, "I want to go now."

Markos regained his breath and staggered back two steps, glaring at me. A chill ran across my shoulders. His stare was brilliant and hard, filled with hatred and something else— confidence. He wasn't hoping for payback; he was sure of it.

Petros hurried to turn me back toward the van, muttering anxiously in Greek. We stepped inside, closed the doors, and the Mercedes roared past us. Petros wiped sweat from his brow, and his lips trembled.

"T-this is bad," he said.

"What's bad?"

But apparently, Petros had exhausted his supply of English. We rode the rest of the way in silence. I wondered about Markos. On his own, no problem. I'd run into plenty of bullies growing up in South Dallas. None of them ever took a second run at a better fighter. But Markos was not alone; he was the driver for someone in a high-end Mercedes.

After a couple miles, we entered the central section of Fira, where a crazy mix of pedestrians, scooters, four-wheelers, cargo trucks, tour buses, and vans like ours slowed traffic to a crawl. Eucalyptus trees grew tall beside the street. Brightly flowering bushes and gardens decorated the alleyways. We passed a small municipal building section, a smattering of tour offices and rental-car agencies, and then turned right to bypass the main part of the tourist town. In another mile, we entered the village of Imerovigli, where I was to stay. Petros turned off the road to wind through small alleys, and we soon came to a tiny parking lot on top of the cliff.

I got out and was transfixed by my first unobstructed view of the caldera. A thousand feet below me, the sea spread out from the base of the cliff until it reached the far horizon. My mind had difficulty comprehending that the sea at my feet was at the same elevation as the sea at the end of the world.

Petros fetched my bag, and I followed him down a steep set of narrow concrete steps. Beneath me, the side of the cliff was filled with the front entryways of small white hotels. Behind the facades, I knew the bedroom suites were carved directly into the cliff wall. A hundred feet farther down, a walkway traversed the side of the cliff, to the left toward Fira and out of view to the right.

Directly in front of me, a small conical peninsula jutted out from the shore. The cone rose nearly to my elevation, had a flat hundred-foot-square section on top, and was connected to the main island by a narrow isthmus. Nea Kameni—the volcanic island—rose from the water a mile offshore.

My hotel—Liakáda Suites—had twenty-four rooms spread across three levels connected by stairwells. Petros and I descended one level to the modest lobby, which contained a simple check-in table with two straight-backed chairs in front and a desktop computer to the side. A woman sat behind the desk staring at the monitor, and a man leaned over her to point at something on the screen. At the noise of our entrance, they both glanced over.

At first, no one moved. The seated woman was in her thirties with fine hair, dark skin, and perfect posture. Her beauty was mesmerizing, simple, yet in some mysterious way transcendent: luminous skin, deep brown eyes, and full moist lips. Was this how Paris of Troy felt when he first beheld Helen? No, probably not, because this woman frowned at me as if I'd interrupted a critical moment.

The man wore a brightly colored shirt, skinny jeans visible under the check-in table, and sparkly golden shoes that might have been worn by an elf. He was a little over five feet and slightly built. He smiled broadly.

"You must be Mr. Robbins," he said, and hurried around the desk to shake my hand. "We are excited to have you stay with us for a while. My name is Constantine. I am the hotel manager."

"Please, call me Joe."

Constantine turned to the woman. "Selene, please check Joe in."

She rubbed the back of her neck and squinted at me. What had I done to her?

"Your passport?" she said, in as icy a tone as I have ever heard from a hotel receptionist.

Constantine raised his eyebrows.

Petros shuffled his feet and made to leave. Jeez, the tip. I scrambled for a ten-euro note and thanked him for the ride.

During the check-in process, I did my best to thaw Selene with lots of pleases, thank-yous, and big smiles, but nothing worked. Too bad. In addition to her lovely face and mannerisms, she had a cute figure. With six weeks of vacation to go, I could use some companionship, a local who knew her way around, but Selene had no interest in getting to know me. She expertly accessed my record from the computer, efficiently entered my passport information, and made it clear that our transaction was complete.

Then Constantine showed me to my room. Along the way, his eyes darted here and there to inspect the hotel premises. On the stairs, he leaned over to retrieve a discarded gum wrapper. While we walked, he described the hotel amenities: how to access the Internet, breakfast hours, maid service, and the other essentials.

The suite resembled an efficiency, with a small stove, refrigerator, and dining table in addition to a sitting area with a television. The bedroom came with a queen-size bed. The bathroom had a large tub with a shower fixture hanging from the ceiling. Two large rock formations—painted black—grew from the wall, a constant reminder that the room was a cave dwelling.

"The best part is the spare room," Constantine reported. "It's small but has its own single bed, which is perfect for a visitor."

"Great."

Outside, he provided more useful information. I could find basic food and drinks at several small grocery shops within easy walking distance. Fira was two miles down the paved walkway that traversed the cliff. In addition to more suites, my level of the hotel contained the outdoor hotel pool and a large patio with lounge chairs for viewing the caldera. The remaining suites occupied the next level down.

Constantine recommended I try a nearby restaurant for dinner. I asked if he would join me, my treat. He seemed a little surprised. I explained that I wanted to learn more about the island and didn't enjoy eating alone. He had plans for the evening but would show me the way to the restaurant and stay for a glass of wine.

We paused on the patio outside my room to look out to sea, and he pointed to the cone-shaped peninsula. "That's Skaros Rock. A stone fortress once stood out there. You can still see the ruins."

A lone hiker strolled on the peak of the rock.

"Have you ever hiked to the top?" I said.

"Me? No. My friends have tried to convince me, but I'm scared of heights. There's a trail that goes up the back, but it's a scramble."

"I'll keep it in mind."

"The peak is sixty meters. A fall would definitely kill you." He grinned. "So don't do that unless you want to commit suicide."

"You bet."

After Constantine left, I unpacked. In addition to basic summer clothes, I had brought several nonstandard items. The first was my Leatherman pocketknife, a tool of many uses. Next, I pulled out my Steiner binoculars, a must-bring suggestion from a blog post I'd read about the views.

Then I searched for a hiding place for my cash. I had brought five thousand US dollars in twenties. ATMs were ubiquitous the world over, and almost everyone accepted plastic, but there were still times when a roll of fifty twenties would arrange miracles. I unzipped one of the couch cushions, took out the foam pillow, and sliced an opening on one side. Then I placed three thousand inside the pillow, sewed the opening closed with a needle and thread from my bathing kit and stuffed the pillow into the case with the opening on the opposite end from the zipper. I put the rest of the cash in the closet safe.

I spent ten minutes surveying the caldera with my binoculars, relaxed poolside with my book for an hour, and then showered for dinner.

Chapter 2

TO GET TO THE WALKWAY, Constantine and I climbed down three flights of stairs. The paved path followed the contours of the cliff and wound between a mix of small stone residences and boutique hotels like the Liakáda. Above us, the cliff rose two hundred feet, and on our right, the waters of the caldera brilliantly reflected the setting sun. We passed a few others on the way, tourists mostly.

"How's your room?" he asked.

"Fine. No issues. And the patio and pool are great."

"Good." He bit the corner of his lip and scraped a hand through his hair. "Hey, I'm sorry Selene was impolite when you checked in. I'll speak to her."

I hadn't given it much thought. She was probably just having a bad day.

"Don't do that on my account," I said. "She's good at what she does."

"I'm afraid Selene dislikes all Americans."

"Yeah? Must be tough with so many of us around."

He shrugged. "Her husband used to pick up American women on cruise ships. More than a few times."

"Oh."

"Now she's a single mother with lots of headaches, scrambling for money and trying to keep her teenage son out of trouble. It's difficult."

"I get it."

"And everyone knows her story. Santorini is a small island. Only twenty thousand people live here in the winter. Everyone knows everyone."

"Okay. Maybe I can show her we're not all bad people."

Constantine nodded, his eyes uncertain, lingering on me long enough that he lost sight of the path and nearly stumbled on a rough spot. He might have been checking me out. I couldn't tell for sure. If he was, I assumed his gaydar would soon tell him I didn't roll his way.

In the twenty minutes it took for us to reach the restaurant, the sun lost five degrees of angle from the horizon, changing the sky's brightness as if the sun god were slowly turning a rheostat. The heat of the day had abated, and a light, refreshing breeze stirred the air.

The restaurant had ten indoor tables and an equal number on the patio. We chose to sit outside to monitor the sunset and the passersby on the walkway. Constantine ordered a Campari and soda, and I selected a half bottle of local wine that would last me through dinner. His reference to the winter population of the island made me wonder what everyone did in the off-season. Would the waters of the caldera sparkle as brightly when cold weather chased the tourists away?

"Do you live here year round?" I asked.

"No." He fanned his hands like a magician announcing a trick. "I go to Paris to work in a fashion boutique on Rue Saint Honoré in the premier arrondissement."

I nodded, and he continued with his story.

"When I first arrived in Paris, I knew nothing of fashion. I worked for a shop for free, folding clothes and cleaning the store. The owner let me sleep in the back. Slowly, I learned. I watched everything, listened, and read the magazines cover-to-cover two and three times. The next year I worked for another shop, and they paid me. That's where I learned about back office systems. I did the daily reports, the bookkeeping, and the nightly deposits. The next year, I got a job at a third shop, this time working as a sales clerk earning a commission."

"Great story," I said. "In Texas, we call that pulling yourself up by your bootstraps."

He laughed. "I like that. And I'm not finished pulling. My dream is to open my own boutique in Paris with clothes inspired by the Mediterranean lifestyle, casual with lots of bright colors."

"Dreams can take you a long way," I said.

"I hope so."

Then I asked Constantine if he could recommend a local guide.

"Oh, yes," he said. "I know of several good services."

"I don't want a traditional guide. I don't need the tutorials on history and architecture, and I can't afford them anyway. I just want an underemployed local who can show me the island."

As he pondered my request, his eyes drifted out to the burnt orange horizon. After a minute's reflection, he sat straighter in the chair.

"I have an idea that might improve your relationship with Selene," he said. "You should hire her son, Julian. Like many kids his age, he has too much time on his hands, and Selene works most days and some nights."

"He's not a brat, is he?"

"What is a brat?"

"A spoiled child. A jerk."

"No. He's a good boy. Sixteen. And he knows the island. Plus, it wouldn't cost you much. Pay him ten euros a day, buy him lunch, and he'll be happy."

"Cool. I'd like to try it."

Constantine said he would call Selene to discuss the idea. He stayed another ten minutes to finish his Campari, then left to join his friends in Fira.

I studied the patrons of the restaurant. More than half appeared to be locals, always a good sign. The air carried the fragrance of carefully mixed spices: garlic, oregano, and a trace of mint. After consulting with my waiter, I ordered a salad and lamb stew with rice. Upon delivering the salad, my waiter—a long-time employee—lingered to explain the history of the restaurant, which had been owned and run by a single family for four generations. After the lamb stew, his insisted I try the baklava, which he claimed was the best in all of Santorini.

I was finishing a cup of coffee when I spied the young American couple from the ferry. The sun had now set, and they were traversing the darkened route from the direction of Fira. Perhaps they were staying at one of the other cliffside hotels in Imerovigli. His eyes stayed glued to his phone as his thumbs tapped on the screen. Meanwhile, in a white summer dress that highlighted her sun-kissed skin, his companion stopped to admire the bougainvillea under the front lights of the restaurant. Tight blond curls framed her otherwise ordinary face. Built like a swimmer—medium height with strong shoulders and arms—she smiled and said something, but her friend had moved ahead out of earshot, so she hurried to catch up.

I wished that Rose and I had visited Santorini at that age. We would have taken long walks while holding hands, sampled the local fare and wine, and made sweet love with the windows open, our hot bodies cooled by the air of the Mediterranean. But in our early twenties, we couldn't afford exotic trips to places like

Santorini. It was all about work and then raising small kids, and then more work, and success, and infidelity.

When I got to the infidelity part, the part that always dragged me down, I signaled the waiter for the check.

Twenty minutes later, I rounded a corner in the walkway to see the full blaze of Fira—a tourist's paradise with restaurants, bars, and hotels clustered in winding streets on top of the cliff. Balconies and patios jockeyed for position to provide the best view of the caldera.

Three oceangoing cruise ships floated in the harbor below, having dispersed their passengers for nightlife and shopping. At the bottom of the cliff, a large docking area accommodated shuttles from the cruise ships and the local tour boats. There were two ways to make the journey from the clifftop to the dock: a funicular and a concrete path used by the famous donkeys of Santorini. For five euros, a passenger could ride a donkey along the narrow switchbacks. A pungent byproduct of the donkey concession lightly scented the breeze.

Rounding another turn, I came upon the Azure, a name I recognized from my guidebook as a casual bar with a fantastic view. The Azure was a small place, with a stone-top bar inside and a balcony with two- and four-seat tables that overlooked the caldera. I grabbed the last bar stool and ordered a martini. Canned reggae music played from hidden speakers, and a lone waitress worked the tables.

On my right, a man and woman studied their phones. An attractive woman on my left wore a casual dress and sipped from a glass of white wine. She nodded at me, and I nodded back.

"American?" she said.

"Yeah. Austin."

She nodded again. "Cool city."

"What about you?"

"I'm from Cincinnati, which is a long way from here in more ways than one."

I got the feeling with a little prompting she would tell her story. "So, are you here on a cruise or something?"

"No. I'm staying two weeks. Just got in today. Came alone. It's a celebration of sorts—the divorce came through. I left the boys with my ex and came here to think about what's next."

She paused, and I didn't want the silence to linger, so I said, "I'm also divorced, but it's been a couple years."

After a quick survey of the room and a glance in the direction of the dark caldera, she turned back to me. "It kinda sucks to be single in a beautiful place like this."

Okay. I didn't know how to respond to that. Was that her pickup line?

She must have seen laugh crinkles around my eyes because she blinked twice, realized how her statement sounded to me, and then burst out laughing.

I laughed along with her.

The laughing made her shoulders shake. She covered her eyes with a hand, embarrassed, then turned to me again. "I promise. I'm not trying to hook up with you."

"No worries."

Her eyebrows pitched up, and she touched my forearm. "Not that that would be a bad thing. I mean . . . you *are* attractive."

My eyes widened, and she broke out laughing again.

"This keeps getting better," I said.

She couldn't stop laughing and soon had to wipe away tears. Her back curled, and she buried her face in her hands. I took the opportunity to check out her legs. Nice. She wore leather sandals with thin straps.

When she started to get things under control, I said, "You're making it too easy for me."

"That was not my intention. Not at all. By the way, I'm Crystal."

We were mirror images in some ways. Crystal had two boys near the same ages as Chandler and Callie. She worked as a freelance artist: graphic design, illustrations, and some voice acting. She liked the freedom that came with not having the same boss day after day. Traveling was a passion she'd never pursued in her marriage due to her husband's predilection for routine.

She had sandy blond hair cut to the shoulders and light blue eyes that smiled often. Her dress fit snugly around her trim waist and revealed enough cleavage to catch my eye.

We stayed for two drinks and then wandered into town to peruse the open-air shops. She bought me a hat, declaring as she tried it on my head, "Tall men on island vacations should always wear a straw fedora." I tried to act the part by strolling casually through the shops. She sauntered a few steps in front of me in a deliciously feminine way. We stopped for a nightcap at a patio bar and made plans.

Crystal rubbed her hands together as if she wished to address a delicate point, then said, "I don't think an affair is in the cards for us."

"Okay."

"I'm not ready for it."

Wow. I had encountered few women as direct as Crystal. No wasting time for her. She knew what she wanted, and what she didn't.

"That's fine," I said. "I didn't expect otherwise. But I hate to eat alone. Perhaps we could explore the island together while you're here."

"I'd like that. But I can't make it tomorrow. I have serious shopping plans."

"No problem. I need to work tomorrow morning."

"Work? I thought this trip was strictly R&R."

"Mostly, but I'm also doing a profit analysis for the owner of my hotel. In exchange, he's giving me a break on the room rate."

"Sweet deal."

"How about dinner tomorrow?" I asked.

She gave me a warm smile for an answer.

After drinks, I accompanied Crystal to her place, a three-story hotel named the Acropolis that was located in the tourist town's center. It had white walls and curved arches over the balconies. At the entrance, she stopped to give me a light hug and then climbed the few steps to the door. Before disappearing inside, she turned, lifted a hand, and wiggled her fingers at me.

With long, energetic strides, I made short work of the hike back to my hotel. A million stars shone above, but no moon, so I had to tread carefully on the unlit sections of the path. I had much to look forward to on my vacation. When I neared Imerovigli, the dark shape of Skaros Rock loomed offshore on my left, challenging me. I resolved that in the morning I would answer the challenge.

Chapter 3

I WOKE EARLY, dressed for a workout, and descended to the walkway. I turned right in the direction of Oia to warm up with a short run before ascending Skaros Rock. The path had numerous changes in elevation and many uneven spots. It made for great exercise, but to avoid a sprained ankle or worse I had to continually study the path ahead, which proved difficult because my eyes begged to wander to the stunning view on my left. Occasionally, I stopped a few moments to study the caldera with its ring of cliffs and deep blue water.

After ten minutes, I turned around to head back, my T-shirt soaked with perspiration. Above me, guests of hotels similar to mine sat outside on patios to enjoy coffee and pastries. On the opposite side, the cliffs gave way to the sea.

The steps down to the isthmus to Skaros made for easy walking, but the path grew harder to follow as it wound around the base of the rock. I scrambled over broken boulders and loose rocks. Once around the back, I had to decide whether the final ascent—a challenge from the sight of it—was worth the risk. The view was already spectacular. Then again, I had seen a guy on the peak the previous day. How hard could it be?

Pretty hard, as it turned out, but I kept three points of contact on the rock surface at all times and clambered up in a few minutes. At the end, I had to reach high with both hands and strain to lift my body weight onto the plateau. Constantine had said his fear of heights kept him away from Skaros Rock, but I doubted he had the strength to make the climb even if he tried.

I ventured to the far side and peered over the edge. A sense of vertigo threatened me, so I took a knee. Yep. A fall from here would be a fatal mistake. It was a sixty-foot drop to the first set of rocks, and the incline at that point remained steep. The rock on the slope was loose and worn into small pieces that resembled shale. If the initial impact didn't kill a person, the subsequent violent tumble through loose rock would finish the job. I stood and took a step back.

We spend our lives struggling to make the good times outnumber the bad. Three easy steps and my struggles would be over for good. A bird of prey cried nearby, circling on the breeze in search of breakfast. I turned around to make my descent.

Upon my return to the hotel, Selene waited for me outside my room. In tight-fitting white jeans and a fuchsia top, her hands fidgeted at her front. Her fine dark hair graced the tops of her shoulders. It was the first time I had seen her out from behind the desk. Whoa. My pulse jumped a beat, and I tried to neutralize my expression, so I wouldn't come across as just another ugly American.

"Good morning," I said.

She pulled on her earlobe and cleared her throat. "Did you have a good run?"

"Yes, it's fantastic early, nice and cool. I climbed Skaros."

She nodded noncommittally but said nothing else, simply stood there barring the entrance to my room.

"Is something wrong?" I said.

"No. Nothing is wrong."

What the heck? Then it hit me. The conversation with Constantine about hiring her son as a guide.

"Sorry. Did Constantine call you?"

"Yes."

"Is it all right? For me to hire your son."

"First, we will discuss the rules."

"Okay."

"Julian is not allowed to drink alcohol with you."

"No. Of course not. What is he? Sixteen?"

"No drugs."

"I don't do drugs."

"And he can't drive."

"I'll drive."

"And *you* can't drink and drive."

Selene clearly didn't trust me. Perhaps this wasn't a good idea after all.

"Look. If you don't want me to hire Julian—"

"No, I do." She put her hands up, anxious that I not misinterpret her questions. "I want you to hire him. This would help me a great deal. Thank you."

I nodded. "All right. Let's do it."

"What time do you want to leave?"

"Noonish. Tell him to bring a bathing suit. We'll get lunch on the way."

Selene's tension melted. Her shoulders relaxed, and for the first time, she smiled at me. "Thank you, Mr. Robbins."

"Please, call me Joe."

"If you need anything while you are in Santorini, come to me. I will help you." She said this with an air of innocence, as one neighbor would speak to another. Selene was prepared to return the favor she thought I had done for her; nevertheless, to clarify her intentions, she said, "But I'm not going to sleep with you."

I nodded again. "That's good to know. It's . . . always good to be clear. I mean . . ." Jeez. What the heck did I mean?

Selene didn't wait for more from me. She turned on her heel, and I watched her cute figure take three steps and turn up the stairs.

It was eight o'clock, and I needed to hustle. I was to meet Giorgos Papadopoulos—the owner of the hotel and my client— for breakfast in thirty minutes.

Chapter 4

IN SHORTS, A T-SHIRT, AND SANDALS, I hiked up one level to where the hotel served breakfast. Giorgos sat under a large umbrella and wore light wool slacks and a long-sleeve business shirt with the collar open. He stood to greet me. He was a large man, taller than me by a couple inches, and barrel-chested with the hard, round stomach typical of men in their fifties who enjoyed both a rich diet and an active lifestyle. I ordered coffee and a full breakfast and sat back to absorb the view: whitewashed abodes on the side of the cliff, deep blue water, Skaros Rock, and the volcanic island in the distance.

"Spectacular, yes?" said Giorgos.

We discussed the view. I asked if he ever got used to it.

"Like eating breakfast," he said. "Most days . . . nothing special. We live with a view and we die with a view. But once in a while, I stop and wonder what I did in a prior life to earn living in such a beautiful place now."

I scanned the panorama again. Austin had some pleasing scenery, but nothing like that.

The food arrived, fresh and hot from the kitchen, and we took a few moments to eat. I had ordered an omelet, sausage, toast, and fruit. Our conversation turned to the profitability of his hotel. Through my earlier video conversations with Giorgos, I had learned that he owned several other businesses in Santorini and that all of them were doing well except for the Liakáda. I had already done market research to determine his room prices were in line with the competition and that the Liakáda was available on the popular online booking sites. To dig in, I needed access to the hotel's records. Fortunately, the hotel systems were now all in the cloud, and Giorgos gave me his admin password, which provided access to everything.

"I don't know the systems," he said. "But Constantine is good with computers. He's brought all of our systems into the cloud in the last two years."

Giorgos went on to explain that Constantine managed the operation and back office for the hotel, while Selene handled marketing and distribution.

"Who compiles the financial reports?"

"Constantine prepares the basics and hands everything over to my bookkeeper."

"Do you trust your bookkeeper?"

"Yes, I've used her for twenty years. She prepares my tax returns and double-checks all the numbers. The only exception to the admin structure for any of the systems is payroll."

"Okay."

"We used to do payroll by hand. When Constantine came to work for me two years ago, he suggested I switch to the system they used at his last company. He is the only authorized user of the payroll system, but I have his password. He and I always review the payroll together before he finalizes it."

He gave me Constantine's password for the payroll system. I was all set to begin the project and told Giorgos I would spend a few hours a day on the work and give him an update the following week.

We had finished breakfast by then, and I thought we would get up to leave, but he had one more item on his list. His demeanor to that point had been friendly, hospitable, but now his face turned darker, with his eyebrows furrowing and his lips in a flat line.

He said, "I understand from Petros that you had some trouble with a local man on the way in from the airport."

With so much going on, I had almost forgotten the incident with Markos. When Giorgos mentioned it, I recalled Markos's facial expression after I knocked the wind out of him.

"Markos," I said. "His name was Markos. It wasn't that big of a thing."

"It's totally unacceptable. I know this Markos. He is not a good person. There are rumors about him and women. Accusations were made but unproven. For him to offend my driver and a client of my hotel, this is a big deal."

No question, Giorgos was angry. It made me wonder again about Markos. Should I worry about him?

Giorgos continued. "Markos works for the son of a good friend of mine, Theo Bakas. As it happens, Theo is the general contractor for a public works project, and his son Dorian has assumed the role of manager. When you came across them yesterday, they were reviewing progress."

I recalled seeing the construction fence and the idle site.

"What's the project?" I asked.

"A major upgrade to the island's wastewater treatment facilities. Santorini is a popular tourist destination. Visitors leave rave reviews, but they also consistently complain about our sewage treatment limitations."

It seemed silly, but Giorgos was right. Due to the limitations of the current system, hotel guests were asked to refrain from flushing toilet paper. Instead, discard bins were placed in bathrooms, a practice unfamiliar to many tourists. I had noticed this complaint often when researching the market.

"The good news," he said, "is that the project will construct new pumping stations, larger transit lines, and a treatment plant with enough capacity for the entire island."

"Big project."

"Yes. Fira will go online before the next tourist season. The rest of the island will follow throughout the year. When the project is complete, we'll have no more complaints."

Hmm. I had called it a big project, but massive was a better adjective. I considered the force required to pump wastewater from the sides of the cliffs to the top and the miles of trenches to be dug and pipes to be laid. To get online in the next year, they'd have to hurry.

"I have spoken with Theo," Giorgos said. "You will have no more trouble from Markos."

"Thank you."

Giorgos glanced to make sure the wait staff was out of earshot.

"In Santorini, we take care of problems in our own way. We like to keep things running smoothly on the island for the tourist trade. This is why I am confident you will have no problem."

"It's a close community," I said.

"Yes."

"I'm getting a feel for it. You have your own style."

"Yes," he said.

"Santorini style," I said.

Giorgos smiled and nodded. "I have never heard it put that way in English, but it's true. We do things Santorini style."

Chapter 5

BACK IN THE ROOM, I pulled out my laptop and logged into the hotel systems using Giorgos's password. Then I took a crash course in hotel economics. They used a cloud-based system called Boutique HMS (Hotel Management System) designed specifically for small hotels. The system provided the front office capability for connecting with online distribution channels, a booking engine, inventory management, and a retail point-of-sale module. It also included functionality for back office management of hotel-staff scheduling, procurement, integration with a financial system for accounts payable, and producing basic management reporting. I had tons of data at my disposal.

The restaurant and bar services provided by the hotel were outside the scope of my project. Giorgos had rolled those operations into a business he owned and managed separately from the Liakáda.

I started on the expense side of the equation by analyzing the trends of primary cost drivers: distribution, advertising and promotion, payroll, laundry, and maintenance. Using the basic reports of the hotel system combined with historical financial statements, I scrutinized cost by category for the last three years. If expenses in any category had risen as a percentage of the top line, it might indicate an operational problem or even fraud. Slack procurement practices could have driven cost increases for supplies or outside services. Fraud could show up in falsified payroll or supplier costs. I found a few small things that I noted for a more detailed review but nothing big enough to cause significant concern. Analyzing those numbers burned most of the morning. I concluded the problem was probably on the revenue side, a more complex world that would have to wait for another day.

I changed into a bathing suit, grabbed a beach towel, and strode into the village to rent a car.

Chapter 6

I RENTED A STANDARD TRANSMISSION Opel Corsa with tiny back seats. The car's small frame would make for easier parking in the crowded lots of Santorini.

Julian met me at the top of the stairs. He was a tall, thin boy with a big nose and an unkempt forest of black hair on his head. In a royal blue bathing suit, white shirt, and sandals, he looked a lot like a tourist kid, except he didn't have a phone. His eyes moved around a lot—to the car, to me, to a girl riding a bike past us on the street, back to me, and then to his feet. Nervous. No worries. We'd get through that part soon enough.

"Where to?" I said.

He lifted his head toward me with his eyebrows squeezed together. We didn't have a lot of time because I needed to return in a few hours to get ready to meet Crystal for dinner.

"I want to go swimming," I said. "What's a good beach?"

"You want to go parasailing? Fishing?"

"Let's go to a beach where they have pretty girls."

He smiled and nodded. We had found a common interest.

"Kamari," he said.

Kamari was on the eastern side of the island. In a straight line, Santorini was only ten miles from end to end, but there was never an easy way to get from here to there.

We retraced the route Petros had taken to drive me from the ferry port the day before. After a few miles, we got caught behind a flatbed carrying a midsize backhoe. I couldn't safely pass him on the two-lane road because of the heavy tourist traffic. Eventually, he slowed at the spot where I'd had the dustup with Markos. The truck turned onto the construction road, and I studied the gate carefully. A large sign contained several Greek words.

"What's that?" I asked to make small talk with Julian.

"This is big project to bring . . . ah . . . the sewage from Fira and other towns to be treated. This is a good thing. This makes Santorini a better island than the others."

Through the fence, I observed two more trucks and six men standing and talking. From what I could see, they hadn't yet broken ground on the treatment plant itself. The fence ran parallel to our road for a hundred yards and then made a ninety-degree turn into the scrub trees.

The people of Santorini had undertaken a big project. The treatment plant itself was fairly straightforward; the challenge was bringing the wastewater to the plant. Moving the waste across rough terrain without the benefit of gravity would require hundreds of miles of underground piping and periodic pumping stations to keep the effluent flowing.

My earlier conversation with Giorgos had me wondering about the project, so on the drive from Fira, I scanned the roadside for crews but saw no one working on the lines or pumping stations. Giorgos had said the system would come online by the next tourist season. I had my doubts, but it wouldn't be the first public works project to finish behind schedule.

A mile later, we turned left and crossed the island to Kamari.

The beach town was optimized to entice money from tourists, with paid parking lots a block from the action and a long pedestrian promenade filled with restaurants, shops, and bars. Restaurants next to the beach rented sunbeds and thatched-roof huts to provide shade. The black sand was so hot they had built wooden walkways onto the beach. We set up camp and waded into the calm sea. Julian pointed to a group of rocks a hundred yards offshore where a dozen people were sunbathing.

"You can swim that far?" he asked.

"Yes."

The water felt cool at first, but I quickly grew used to it. Julian was a clumsy swimmer, all enthusiasm and no finesse. It took us a few minutes to get there, and after pulling ourselves onto a flat section of the rocks, we both breathed heavily.

The sunbathers were all tourists, young adults from the world over. Twenty feet from us, three American girls self-consciously experimented with topless sunbathing. Julian watched them without embarrassment. Two of them had the perky breasts of the young. The third was a big woman with large breasts that lay heavy against her chest.

He turned to me, and his eyebrows danced a couple times.

"I like the big ones," he said.

I respected a man who knew his tastes at such a young age. Me? Sitting on the rocks with the sun drying my skin, I liked them all.

After swimming back, we ate lunch at one of the restaurants on the promenade. Julian had begun to relax around me. He told me about growing up in Santorini. He was bored with life in such a small place. When he reached the legal age of adulthood, he would move to Athens to become a singer in a rock band. He had big dreams, like Chandler and Callie. For the young, life was an endless parade of opportunity.

Outside the restaurant, a black Mercedes sedan had parked on the other side of the pedestrian-only promenade. Apparently, the owner believed he was privileged enough to flout the rules. Julian glanced at the car and then quickly looked away. With the dark windows, I couldn't tell whether anyone was inside.

"You know that car?" I asked.

"Everyone in Santorini knows that car. It belongs to Dorian Bakas." Julian kicked a pebble. "The Bakas family are a big deal here."

"So I gather."

The window of the Mercedes glided down, and Markos, the driver, leaned out with an obnoxious smile on his face. He said something in Greek and then quickly rolled the window up again.

It seemed an odd coincidence that Dorian Bakas and I should choose the same day to visit the beach at Kamari. Were he and Markos following me? No. Surely not.

Julian and I ambled along the promenade in the direction of the parking lot.

"What did he say?" I asked.

"Have a good day."

Curious. Have a good day? The chill I'd experienced the day before returned to my shoulders. Markos was a strange man, not properly tuned in the balance department, anger issues and whatnot.

"Actually," said Julian, "what he said was, 'Enjoy your evening,' but I made a slight change in the translation."

On the drive back, Julian and I made plans to visit a different part of the island the next day. I'd bring Crystal along if she was free. We rolled the windows down and turned on the radio to listen to Greek rock music. Julian interpreted the lyrics for me, but I could scarcely pay attention, distracted as I was by the memories of Crystal's laugh and how she had waved at me from the door of her hotel.

Chapter 7

I arrived at Crystal's hotel at 6:15—fifteen minutes early—and ordered a beer in the lobby bar. Decorated upscale, the bar had a glossy hardwood top and was fully stocked with high-end liquors. Happy patrons sipped early-evening cocktails and discussed their island adventures of the day. Jazz music played softly from overhead speakers. The one waitress moved soundlessly between the six four-top tables.

I stretched the beer to last until 6:40, allowing her the ten-minute cushion that all women are entitled to without question. Then I sent a text saying I was in the lobby. No immediate response.

I ordered some nuts and a second beer. She must have enjoyed the shopping. Perhaps she was still in the shower.

At 6:50 I grew concerned. Had she ghosted me? Decided the six-four Texan was all hat and no cattle? Moved on to Mykonos, where the guys were younger and the action hotter? I called her mobile, got voice mail, but didn't leave a message.

Seven o'clock came and went. No big deal. She'd been delayed, and her mobile battery had died. But by 7:15, my imagination began to run a little wild. She'd fallen in the shower, hit her head, and required emergency assistance. She'd had an allergic reaction to shellfish she'd eaten for lunch and now lay helpless in bed, too weak to retrieve her phone from the bureau. Someone had stolen her purse, and she was still filing the police report.

Oddly enough, I knew the location of her room. When we approached the hotel the previous night, she had pointed it out—second floor, third room from the end.

I leaned toward the bartender and told him I'd return in a few minutes. Then I hurried into the main lobby and climbed the stairs at the side. My heart picked up speed as I counted three rooms from the end. Room 218 had an off-white door with a peephole.

I knocked as if nothing were out of the ordinary and waited for thirty seconds. With no response, I knocked louder. I put my ear to the door and heard a Greek folk song, perhaps coming from a radio. The tambourine urged the string player to play faster.

I pounded on the door to remove any doubt in Crystal's mind that someone wanted her attention. The door across the hall opened. A man in a robe squinted at me, set his room service tray on the floor, and closed his door again. Still no answer from Crystal.

With a racing heart, I descended the stairwell two steps at a time and hurried to the front desk. Dressed in a short navy coat with a white shirt and black tie, the clerk stood attentively behind his monitor. My chest heaved. He raised his eyebrows at my urgent approach.

"This will sound strange, but I was supposed to have dinner with a guest of the hotel, and she is nearly an hour late."

"I'm sorry to hear that, sir," he said without emotion.

"I went to her room and knocked on the door. She didn't answer, but I can hear music playing in the room. I'm concerned that she may be sick and need help."

He studied my face. High-end hotels offered confidentiality as a basic amenity and denied visitors from accessing guests without explicit permission. But my expression must have compelled the clerk to take action.

"What is the name of the guest, sir?"

"Crystal."

"Last name?"

Jeez, had she given me her last name? Yes, I had noted to myself that it started with the same letter as Robbins. But it was German, not English. "Reiter. Crystal Reiter. Room 218."

"And your name?"

"Robbins. Joe Robbins."

He dialed Crystal's room, and I hoped against lost hope that she would answer. But she didn't. The clerk's face began to show real concern. He called another number, and in quick Greek chatter, delivered information and instructions.

After hanging up, he said, "One of the ladies from housekeeping will join me at the room. We will open the door, and housekeeping will check to make sure Ms. Reiter is okay."

"I'm coming with you."

"No sir, I'm afraid that's not allowed."

"I'm still coming."

I leaned over the counter, conveying my conviction with my expression and the taut muscles in my arms.

He grabbed his master card key and skipped the elevator in favor of the stairs. At the door, he knocked soundly and called for Crystal by her last name. The woman from housekeeping arrived, clearly nervous. The clerk spoke to her in Greek in a kind but forceful tone. The woman nodded that she understood, and the clerk turned to open the door.

Suddenly, I hoped Crystal wasn't in the room, that she would appear at the top of the stairs, all bubbly, delivering a perfectly logical explanation for her delay.

The woman took tentative steps through the doorway.

"Ms. Reiter?"

The bathroom was on the immediate right, and the housekeeper glanced that way.

"Ms. Reiter?"

She took two more steps, turned her head toward the main part of the room, and gasped. She stood still, her eyes bulging, and her hands began to tremble.

I pushed past the clerk and into the room.

Crystal lay lifeless and naked on the bed.

Behind me, the clerk said, "Oh," and blood rushed to my head. The pounding in my ears drowned out the sound of the music. My eyes went blind, shutting out the horrible scene. I stood that way for several seconds and then grew dizzy and felt as if I might fall. I put my hand to the bed for support and sat on it. The clerk struggled to breathe.

I rushed to check her wrist for a pulse and knew she was dead from the lack of warmth. She lay on her back with her arms and legs tied to the bedposts. She'd been gagged with a hand towel, and her head was angled toward her shoulder, her eyes closed. The only blood showing was a dried trickle from the corner of her mouth, but her neck was grossly discolored.

She's been strangled.

The housekeeper remained silent, but the clerk was hyperventilating. He cleared his throat and said, "What . . ."

"Call the police," I said.

"What?"

I stood and turned toward them. "Step into the hall and call the police. I'll stay here."

He dialed a number on his cell, and they walked out. I sat on the bed again and put my hand on Crystal's side. Her skin felt smooth and well cared for, her body not quite stiff. I wanted her to be warm all over and alive again. I wanted to untie her and cover her with a blanket, but I couldn't disturb the crime scene. I wanted to find who killed her and strangle him myself.

I had taken a vow to do that once—exact revenge—but that was for a close friend, and I barely knew Crystal. That time, I had nearly gotten myself killed, *and* I had lost Rose for good.

In my heart, I knew who had murdered Crystal. I closed my eyes and saw the look on Markos's face after I beat him on the side of the road. He was confident he would get payback.

Don't jump to conclusions. For once, let the police do the work.

Chapter 8

THE FIRST TWO policemen arrived within five minutes. They knew enough to not touch anything. One of them guarded the door to keep onlookers out, and the other kept an eye on me. Over the next twenty minutes, another dozen uniformed officers appeared, each stepping inside to take in the gruesome spectacle. Some of them left and some stayed. The ones who stayed spoke Greek quietly. Invariably, a newcomer would eye me with suspicion, perhaps speculating that I had done the deed, but then the original two officers would explain my presence, and the newcomer would leave me alone. It was a gossip fest. Word of Crystal's murder would spread quickly from street to street, expanding from Fira to the outlying villages, all the way to Oia in the north and the beaches and towns on the outer edge. By the morning, everyone in Santorini would know that an American woman had been strangled.

Finally, a photographer arrived with a superior who shooed everyone else out. The superior wore lightweight pants and a dark sport coat, was in his late thirties or early forties, and was built like a gymnast, compact with powerful legs and light on his feet. His hair was jet black and wavy, and his eyes methodically canvassed the room. He examined Crystal first, walked around the bed to inspect the knots and stared at her face and neck from a close distance. He quickly scanned the rest of her body, paying close attention to her pubic region and upper thighs. Then his eyes darted around the room as if taking inventory of the furniture, Crystal's discarded clothes on the floor, and the shopping bags on the bureau, which I hadn't noticed until that moment. After checking the bathroom over, he said something to the photographer, who began taking pictures. Then the superior approached me.

His eyes examined things with a calm intensity, and I became the subject of a quiet analysis going on inside his mind, a one-man debate with conclusions I would never know unless he wanted me to.

"Your name is Mr. Robbins?" he said.

"Yes."

"Please come with me."

We stepped into a room the police had commandeered three doors down the hall. He offered me a seat in a cushioned chair and sat across from me on the bed. His eyes studied me again as he searched for the right words.

"I'm sorry this happened."

I nodded.

He introduced himself as Captain Veggos, a direct report to the chief of police.

"How do you know Ms. Reiter?"

"I don't know her well."

I explained how I had met Crystal and our plans for the evening. The captain probed me for information on Crystal. I told him everything I knew, but none of it seemed relevant to her being murdered. She knew no one in Santorini and had only arrived the previous day. Veggos continued to ask questions. Every once in a while, he would wrinkle his nose, as if he didn't like the smell of my answer, or perhaps he was annoyed that I gave him nothing that would help solve the murder, or maybe he suspected me. He began asking the same questions again.

"Tell me everything you did in the hotel today."

"We already covered that."

Veggos shrugged.

"We were to meet at six-thirty. I arrived early and waited in the lobby bar. The bartender will remember me. I still haven't paid my bill."

"When did you go to the front desk?"

"First, I went upstairs to knock on her door."

"How did you know her room number?"

"I told you."

Veggos wrinkled his nose, so I went through it all again, step by step. Eventually, he moved on to my activities from earlier in the day. I described my workout, the breakfast meeting with Giorgos, and the day trip with Julian. He asked how long I had worked alone in my room. He wanted to know the exact times. I could imagine his logic trail. I said I had worked for three hours, and he might have believed that was long enough for me to hike to Fira, strangle Crystal, and return in time to rent the car in Imerovigli. I could predict his next steps. He would have officers interview the hotel staff and show my passport photo around to find out if anyone had seen me earlier in the day. And he would direct his team to go through the hotel videos.

He paused longer between questions, staring to the side at nothing to run through his mental notes, trying to sort out what he'd missed. If no one on the island knew Crystal except me, then I was the logical suspect. Any experienced detective would scoff at the notion that a random murderer had marched into the

Acropolis Hotel, talked his way into Crystal's room, and strangled her on the second day of her visit.

No, I was the prime suspect. The fact that I had alerted the clerk to the situation didn't mean I hadn't committed the murder. Perhaps that was my attempt to throw investigators off the trail. But it would take a cold-blooded murderer to perform such a ruse. Which explained why the captain had already spent an hour with me. He wanted to get inside my brain.

"Ms. Reiter was probably raped," he said.

"How do you know that?"

"There are marks on her legs that indicate a struggle. I've seen them on other victims."

Why did he tell me that? Did he wish to see my face turn dark with anger? My blood boiled. I breathed heavily and looked down. My hands were clenched in fists.

Veggos saw them too. He wrinkled his nose.

"I have a lead for you," I said.

He frowned. "Tell me."

I described my altercation with Markos the day before.

Veggos formed a steeple with his fingers and tapped the steeple against his lips.

"So you think Markos—a driver for the Bakas family— discovered Ms. Reiter was a friend of yours and killed her because he was angry with you."

"Yes. At least, it's conceivable."

Veggos wrinkled his nose twice. He found my hypothesis odorous.

"Thank you," he said. "Any other thoughts?"

"No."

"Let me make one observation. I don't know the Bakas family personally, but they have a reputation on Santorini. Theo Bakas is powerful. I advise you to stay clear of them. Don't do anything to follow up on your theory. I'll check it out."

"Sure. Thanks."

Veggos went on to explain the procedure going forward. Few murders occurred on Santorini, and the police force could not handle all aspects of the investigation. He would oversee the operation locally and act as liaison with experts from the mainland. Crystal's body would be flown to Athens for an autopsy.

Under the guise of making conversation, I asked a couple questions and learned that unlike most of the local police force, Captain Veggos was not a native of Santorini.

"I'm from Athens," he said. "I'm on a two-year rotation. It's part of our federal program to keep career officers familiar with life in the outlying areas of the country."

"I see."

"It puts me at something of a disadvantage on occasion."

"How's that?"

"The local citizens, including the police, don't completely trust me. They have their own way of doing things here."

Santorini style.

Veggos began to wrap up the conversation. He took my number, promised he'd be in touch, and then covered his final point.

"I want to confirm," he said, "that you plan to be here for six weeks."

"Yes," I said, "but I'll stay longer if necessary."

He scrunched his eyebrows.

"I'm not leaving Santorini until you solve the case."

Chapter 9

VEGGOS ARRANGED FOR a uniformed policeman to drive me to my hotel in Imerovigli. Apparently, Fira was abuzz with rumors, and a small crowd had formed in front of the Acropolis. The policeman ushered me through a back entrance and straight into his car.

After he dropped me off, I walked to the local store for a liter of Jack Daniels and a pizza. I stopped by the lobby to ask Constantine for ice. He'd already heard about the murder and my involvement, and he offered me company.

Sitting on lounge chairs around the pool, we ate the pizza, drank a few sour mashes, and gazed at the million stars above the darkened caldera.

Though he must have been terribly curious, Constantine asked me no questions. Instead, he played the role of the empathetic listener. I didn't feel like discussing the murder, so I told him about my kids, Chandler and Callie, about Chandler's bravery in the face of my divorce and Callie's enthusiasm for anything and everything. I recounted vacations we'd taken as a family to destinations less remarkable than Santorini but even more fun. I told him I'd ruined my chance to enjoy any more family vacations and that at times it was hard to muster the strength to breathe.

"It sounds to me like you've paid enough of a price," he said.

"How's that?"

"Lay the guilt down and keep moving. Leave it behind you."

"It sounds easy, but . . ."

"No life is easy," he said. "Believe me. I know this. Even in a society as old as Greece, people still regard me without tolerance. I can let it stop me, or I can keep walking. What does the world care? The caldera will remain as beautiful. The food in Paris is still as delightful. I choose to live."

Constantine was a wise man for someone so young, and smart enough to know that if he had another sour mash, he'd fight a headache in the morning, so he bid me goodnight.

I stayed up late and watched the stars move across the sky. In Cincinnati, two boys and an ex-husband faced a long road of grief. Compared to theirs, my problems were as easy to scale as Skaros Rock. I felt guilty about my self-pity. I was in paradise enjoying myself and working for a client. I had credit in my pocket and cash stuffed inside a pillow in my room.

In the morning, I'd get back to work on the profitability analysis, and soon I would continue to explore the island.

I would let Captain Veggos do his job without interference. But I wouldn't forget the expression on Markos's face after I beat him on the street. And as I toured the island from end to end, I would watch for Markos. Sooner or later, I would come across him again, and then I would walk up close to him, peer into his eyes, and find what lay within.

Chapter 10

AFTER A LATE BREAKFASt, I opened my laptop and resumed the profitability analysis. My work on the cost side had failed to determine the root cause of the problem, but before moving on to revenues, I wanted to examine the quasi-cost category of taxes. Hotel taxes are a cost to the customer but not an expense of the business per se. Taxes are added on to the bill, collected by the hotel, and remitted to the taxing authority.

My trend analysis indicated that total sales taxes collected had increased nineteen percent on a year-over-year basis. A closer inspection revealed that a new fee (labeled Special Utility Tax) of four euros per room night had been added to each customer's bill. I could find no reference to this tax online and called Giorgos to ask him about it.

"That's a special tax to pay for the new wastewater treatment plant. Every hotel and restaurant on the island pays a fair share. The government and trade groups negotiated the tax. I was on the committee. I can't believe that is causing my profitability shortfall."

"I doubt it is. I've ruled out obvious cost problems and am now focusing on the revenue side."

"Do you have everything you need?"

"Yes, the files are well organized."

"Good. Constantine set them up. He's good at this sort of thing. He also works for other hoteliers and businesses on the side to make extra money."

"He's industrious," I said.

"Yes, a hard worker. He might be very successful one day, except . . ."

"Except what?"

The phone went silent, as if Giorgos had said something he wished he hadn't.

"Nothing," he said. "I heard you were somehow involved in this murder of the American."

Jeez. Everyone knew everyone's business in Santorini.

"I knew the victim briefly."

"Are the police treating you well? Do I need to call someone?"

"No. I'm fine. I met with the investigating officer, and he seems competent."

"Okay. Don't feel like you need to work on my project now. It can wait."

"Actually, it's a welcome distraction."

Which was true. After Giorgos hung up, I turned my attention to the revenue side of the equation. At a high level, I discovered the problem almost immediately. The average nightly room rate had increased one to two percent in each of the last three years. However, the occupancy rate—the percentage of available rooms filled on average—had declined almost four percent on a year-over-year basis. Could the higher tax have led to a decrease in met demand? Theoretically, yes, but Giorgos had already informed me that his hotelier friends were earning higher profits than the prior year. So, why were fewer customers booking stays at the Liakáda?

There were many possible suspects: poor service could drive bad reviews that would in turn affect bookings, insufficient presence on the online travel sites, uncompetitive rates, lower repeat sales due to a lack of outreach to prior customers, etc.

First, I considered the quality angle. Based on the service delivered to me, I would give the Liakáda a solid review. Even so, I spent some time preparing an analysis of online reviews. I compared Liakáda's ratings on TripAdvisor with those of the other boutique hotels in Imerovigli. The Liakáda's were better than average. Then I surveyed the review scores on the top five travel sites for Greece. Again the ratings for the Liakáda measured up to the competition. I ruled out quality as the primary driver to lower occupancy.

Next, I reviewed the breadth of Liakáda's presence on third-party online booking sites. One of the primary features of the Boutique HMS software Liakáda used was that it provided automated links to over four hundred sites. A quick scan of the implementation showed that Selene had taken full advantage of the distribution breadth offered by the system.

I reviewed Liakáda's presentation on the top five sites. The photos of the facility were good, the views of the caldera excellent, and the descriptions of amenities succinct and clear. All fine so far. I perused the Liakáda website and compared it to the competition in Imerovigli. The layout was clean, and the booking engine was easy to use.

I delved further into the pricing analysis. A five percent premium to the market could drive customers to other hotels, but the more in-depth analysis verified my earlier quick review: the Liakáda's pricing was competitive.

I rubbed my face. I'd been staring at a screen for three hours and eliminated a few possible sources of the revenue decline, but like a jigsaw puzzle with a thousand small pieces, this problem would take multiple sessions to solve.

I grabbed my binoculars and went outside to take a long look at the caldera. A huge cruise ship steamed toward Fira, and I studied the layout of the decks. Two hikers had climbed to the top of Skaros Rock and were enjoying a picnic lunch. A day trip had docked at Nea Kameni and was disembarking tourists for the hike up the volcano.

By then it was one o'clock. I had arranged to meet Julian near his home in the town of Oia at the northern tip of the island. After a late lunch, he gave me a tour of Oia, which was built on top of the cliff with a spectacular view of the Aegean to the west. Behind Fira, Oia was the second largest tourist destination on the island, with hundreds of shops and eateries on little cobblestone roads that crisscrossed through the village. The heat of the day made my shirt stick to my sides, and we stopped for a cold drink at a cliffside café. As the sun slid toward the horizon, hundreds of tourists lined the walkway that bordered the edge of the cliff. The crowd was in a festive mood, on holiday with friends, witnessing a spectacular demonstration of natural beauty. The sun sank lower, and the surface of the sea glowed with its reflection. The white walls of the town mellowed with the dying rays.

Crystal and I might have sat at that same café to celebrate our serendipitous meeting, but she was in a cold dark place in Athens and would never see the sun again. I was a glum companion for the kid and took him home before the sun had completely set. Back in Imerovigli, Captain Veggos was waiting for me at the hotel.

Chapter 11

H E WAS SITTING ALONE at one of the patio tables next to the pool. Darkness had nearly descended, and a single spotlight from the roof of the hotel cast the captain in a soft light. His coat lay draped over the back of his chair. I sat next to him, and after pleasantries, he got right to it.

"We have solved the crime," he said.

"It was Markos. Wasn't it?"

"No. It was a passenger from one of the cruise ships in town yesterday."

No. Not possible.

I sat back, stunned. Subconsciously, I had been so sure my altercation with Markos had sparked the chain of events leading to Crystal's death, I couldn't immediately grasp that someone else had committed the act. A cruise passenger?

"How?" I said. "Why?"

"One of our first steps in the investigation was to alert the security teams on the ships that visited Santorini yesterday. Early this morning, a report came in from the *Siren of the Seas* that on the way to Athens last night, one of their male passengers jumped overboard to commit suicide."

"Suicide?"

"Yes. My officers had already spent hours going through video from the hotel." The captain wrinkled his nose. "Frankly, the videos were disappointing. They only have three cameras, and of those, only the one trained on the front entrance works. Nevertheless, this morning, we received a photograph of the passenger and were able to match him on the video."

I rubbed my chin. "That doesn't seem like conclusive evidence."

"Let me finish. Ms. Reiter entered the hotel loaded with shopping bags shortly after one o'clock. The cruise passenger followed close behind her. We think he talked his way into her room almost immediately and then strangled her. That would fit the preliminary time of death."

"Did someone witness him going up the stairs or knocking on her door?"

"No, unfortunately."

"Maybe he just came in for a drink."

"The bartender did not see him, but the girl in the gift shop did, and there's more."

My chair creaked as I shifted my weight. Veggos glanced at my bobbing knee, and I put my hand down to still it.

"At eleven o'clock last night, two passengers on the ship witnessed the man jump over the side. It took twenty minutes to turn the ship around. They turned on floodlights to search the sea, but nobody was found. A bartender on the ship reported having a disturbing conversation with the man earlier. The man babbled about murder and rape and having to pay the price. The bartender had another crewman escort the man back to his room and thought no more of it until he heard about the suicide."

It was incredible, such a totally random and tragic way to die, to be caught in the twisted headlights of a mentally ill psychopath.

"But how did he talk his way into her room?"

"The gift shop clerk waited on him. He bought flowers. He might have used them as a ruse, pretending to be with a delivery service."

He must have followed Crystal through the streets and into the hotel. Somehow he determined her room number. Perhaps he rode the elevator with her and turned right after she turned left. He kept an eye on her until she entered her room, and then he went downstairs to buy flowers. Crystal would have guessed they were from me. Who could resist accepting flowers from a new acquaintance? Wait.

"I didn't see any flowers in the room," I said.

"He must have taken them."

The captain's face betrayed his belief that a random stranger had killed Crystal. I had to agree, although I didn't admit that to the captain. The circumstantial evidence was overwhelming: the timing, the flowers, the conversation with the bartender on the ship, and the suicide. There is no good way to die, but this . . . sheesh . . . it would leave holes in her sons' hearts for a long time.

"The US officials will make additional inquiries in his home city. If nothing else turns up, we will close the investigation. In the meantime, I must ask that you remain in Santorini."

"Sure. I'm not going anywhere."

Chapter 12

I SLEPT FITFULLY that night and woke early. I went for a jog halfway to Oia and back on the path that rimmed the cliff. I hoped it would clear my head so I could continue the analysis for Giorgos. It didn't. My mind returned to the image of Crystal's corpse even more than the day before. Perhaps I'd been in a state of shock that kept me from ruminating on the recent trauma, but now the shock had worn off.

I had called Chandler and Callie at their home in Colorado the previous night. Hearing their voices assured me of their safety. As usual, Callie enthusiastically enumerated their recent activities: hiking, swimming, and making cookies. Chandler detected something in my tone. "What's wrong?" she had said. "You sound worn out, flat." I had straightened in the chair and endeavored to animate my words. "It's only jet lag. I'll get over it soon. This place is awesome."

As I neared Imerovigli on the return from my workout, I deliberately stopped to take in the early morning view. It was as delightful as the day I'd arrived, the azure blue of the sky competing for supremacy with the deep blue of the sea, but the immediacy of grief and loss stole the emotion from the landscape. I kicked at the dirt and turned away.

Back at my hotel, I ordered cold cereal delivered to my room. After eating, I opened my laptop and stared at the numbers for ten minutes, but I couldn't summon the will to do the work. The emptiness of my room depressed me, and I decided to walk to Fira. On the way out, I glanced at the straw fedora Crystal had bought me on the night we met. Taking a deep breath, I reached for the hat and placed it on my head.

* * *

UPON REACHING FIRA, I wondered if the locals might recognize me. By now, they must have all heard about the murder of the American woman, and many of them knew about me. But they couldn't know what I looked like. Could they? I adjusted the hat to cover more of my face. They couldn't see my eyes behind the sunglasses, but at my height, it was hard to blend in anywhere.

I hunched my shoulders and wandered through the narrow alleyways filled with shops, then I stopped for a coffee at a café with a dozen outdoor tables. The air had warmed into the high seventies, and the umbrella provided refreshing shade from the bright sun.

As I waited for my latte, I recognized the young American couple from the ferry sitting a few tables away. They engaged in a quiet but earnest argument. The young man was darkly tanned, physically fit, and had an attractive face. He wore cargo shorts, an orange quick-dry T-shirt, and sandals. He made his points calmly and quickly, using animated hand gestures. From that distance, I couldn't make out his words, but I got the impression he was intelligent and articulate.

I remembered the woman's curly blond hair from the ferry but now had a chance to observe her more carefully. She wore running shoes, a simple mauve short-sleeved shirt, and a denim skirt cut at the knees. The sun had tanned her skin, and her necklace resembled others I had seen in the shops in Fira.

The muscles in her shoulders and face were tense. With her knees together, she held her hands in her lap until he said something she found disagreeable, and then she jabbed a finger at his face and dressed him down with sharp words.

He ignored her rebuttal and continued with his spiel. Thirty seconds went by and she jabbed at him again. This happened a few more times, and her voice grew louder. I still couldn't make out the words, but I lip-read her delivering f-bombs and other gems of expression. And then she took her finger out of his face and pointed away from the café, back in the direction of Imerovigli.

The man shrugged and put his hands to the side as if to say, "Seriously?"

She pointed again and answered in words loud enough for me to hear. "Go away!"

The man shook his head and said a few more words. He stood and bent to kiss her on the lips, but she turned her face away, and he settled for the top of her head. When she didn't respond, he left the café.

My latte came, but I barely noticed, for I watched mesmerized, as after the brave battle, she steadily fell apart. At first, she stared straight ahead with a determined set to her jaw, but then her lips began trembling, and she wiped at her eyes. She pressed her face into her hands and leaned forward.

I felt heavy in the chair, emotionally drained. My heart rate slowed to a crawl.

The waiter stopped to ask the blonde a question, but she continued to hide her face, and he grew uncertain, his eyes darting left and right for help, and then he left her alone.

I tried to ignore her without success.

Should I try to do something? No. Leave her be. She's an adult.

That notion lasted thirty more seconds as her shoulders began to shake.

Oh, hang it all.

I carried my latte to her table, sat next to her with confidence, and didn't say a word. I took off my hat and sunglasses and waited. She had no choice but to acknowledge my presence eventually.

"What's your problem?" she said.

I raised my hands in surrender. "I come in peace. I witnessed your heated one-on-one and thought I'd touch base with a fellow American. Like, make sure you're okay."

"I'm fine."

"Cool."

But she didn't look fine. The water brimmed at her lower eyelids. She was only a few moments from a meltdown.

"Another cup of coffee?" I ventured.

Her eyes searched my face, and I tried to make it as unassertive as possible. After studying my eyes, she wiped the tear trails from her cheeks and gave me a little nod, so I signaled the waiter.

For a long while, I talked nonstop about innocuous nonsense: my disagreement with the current structure of NCAA football championship playoffs, stuff like that. After ten minutes of me babbling, she began to relate her story.

"Matt and I have been traveling for six weeks. We both have one more year of grad school, and this trip was supposed to be our test run, like, to see if we're ready to go long term."

I nodded and said, "Got it."

"Things were okay until the last few days. Then Matt started saying he wanted us to split up for a while so we could each do some exploring on our own."

I adopted my empathetic tone and said, "So he's decided he needs some space."

"Yes!" Her face turned red. She had a temper to avoid. "He's such a shit! He doesn't want space; he wants another girl. Between the dark beauties in Italy and Greece and the underclass backpackers, his head's been on a swivel."

I listened while she criticized his inconsiderate behavior: they'd had to go to the museums he wanted to see and take the train that he wanted to take and eat at his preferred restaurants.

"This morning he kept going on about splitting while all the time he's checking out babes left and right. Finally, I told him to eff off."

"I think I saw that part."

"I told him to get his stuff and clear out of the room."

"So that's what he's doing now? Packing his stuff?"

"He'd better be."

"Okay. How about we have an early lunch. There's a place for crepes only a block away."

She glanced at her purse, perhaps considering whether crepes fit her budget.

"On me," I said.

Now she squinted at me. Who was the tall Texan with a two-day beard anyway? Could she trust me?

"I'm hungry," I said, "and I don't like to eat alone."

As we picked up her stuff and made to leave, I thought, *What are you doing?* I'm not the hovering type that's always on the lookout for lost children to help. But she was off balance after the breakup with Matt. And honestly, I could use the distraction. I could go back to my room and spend another two days on Giorgos's problem, but it didn't interest me at the moment. I had no romantic inclinations whatsoever. She was an adult and attractive in a fresh active-lifestyle way, but she was closer in age to Chandler than she was to me. At a certain age gap, younger becomes too young.

Her name was Annie Quarles, and she was ravenous. The tension of the last few days with Matt might have stolen her appetite, but now that the fight was over, it returned. She ate two stuffed crepes, a large smoothie, and a fruit yogurt for dessert.

During the meal, we shared our recent histories. Annie and Matt had landed in London, spent a week in Paris, another two weeks in Italy, and then moved on to Greece. She had heard about the murder of the American woman and was horrified to learn I had known the victim. I rushed on from that gruesome topic to tell her about my girls. She smiled as I bragged about Chandler's academic record and Callie's abilities on the soccer field.

When the check came, Annie watched nervously as I glanced at the numbers and reached for my credit card.

"Are you sure you don't want to split it?" she said.

"No, I insist."

"Truth is," she said, "money will be tight now that I'm picking up the room myself."

I adopted a neutral expression and waited for her to elaborate.

"Matt's family is wealthy. I couldn't afford the trip on my own, but he said he would pay for more than half. I can handle a few weeks, but then I'll have to reroute my flight home and cut the trip short."

"Hey," I said. "I can offer you a cheap tour this afternoon."

I explained my arrangement with Julian and said she was welcome to join the party. I already had a car and Julian's deal was fixed, so there was no extra cost.

With crossed arms, she tilted her head and squinted at me.

I shrugged and said, "Totally your call. I'm trying to be helpful, but Julian's a good kid. You should give it a try."

A smile crept onto her face, and she nodded. "I'm down with that."

When we reached the hotel pool, I spotted Julian in a lounge chair. After I made introductions, he barely glanced at Annie and then stared at his feet. Poor kid. The boy was a natural charmer of girls his age. I had seen him working the local teenagers on the promenade in Kamari, a lady-killer in the making. But conversing with a live-in-the-flesh American woman ten years his senior— that was a different kind of calamari.

Using her fingers, Annie brushed her hair out from the back of her head. Then she took lotion from her day bag and applied it to her arms.

"What's up, Julian?" she said.

He rattled off a few sentences that sounded coherent, but I wouldn't know for sure because he spoke in Greek.

I laughed and gestured for him to stop talking. When he realized his mistake, his face flushed, and I bailed him out by saying, "So, Julian, where should we go this afternoon?"

Chapter 13

WE BECAME AN UNLIKELY trio: the tall Texan, the young blonde, and the local kid. Over the next week, we undertook excursions many tourists never do. We toured the ruins at the top of Mesa Vouno, perused the shelves of Atlantis Books in Oia, and climbed the paths of Pyrgos to see a castle, a church, and what Julian claimed was the best view on the island.

After the third day, once she had grown to trust me, Annie asked if she could move into my spare bedroom and split the cost of the suite to save money.

"Are you sure?" I said. "I could be a slasher."

"So could I," she said. "Ever think about that?"

"No. Honestly, I haven't."

"What do you think?"

What did I think? The suite was big enough. We'd have to share the bathroom, but I didn't spend much time getting ready anyway.

When I didn't answer right away, she said, "Just to be clear, this is a platonic friendship, right?"

"Oh, absolutely. Yeah. Platonic. Certainly."

I still thought of her as a kid a little older than my girls, though in fact, she was a *lot* older than my girls. Even so, sex had not crossed my mind.

"How about we try it a couple days?" she said. "See how it goes."

"Okay, but I won't take your money. I'm incurring the cost already."

"No," she said. "That's not right."

"I insist. You can help with the meals but not the room. I have no student loans and make a good living."

Annie reluctantly agreed. We moved her stuff in later that day, and at first, the arrangement worked out fine.

At night, Annie and I explored restaurants and bars in Fira and Oia. We poked around in small shops hidden in alleys where the clerks spoke little English. We sampled the seafood restaurants in Ammoudi Bay at the base of the cliff in Oia. We stayed out later than I was used to, having a coffee after dinner and then exploring the nightspots.

As a graduate student, this was a natural cadence for Annie. If we rolled into our apartment at two, she could sleep eight hours and wake refreshed. But as the father of children and a veteran of corporate life, I had lost the ability to sleep in long ago.

One morning, I woke around seven—late for me—and got dressed for a run. Annie would sleep another two hours at least. I ran halfway to Oia and back, and the crisp sea air cleared my head. Hiking up the stairs to my apartment, I came across Selene straightening lounge chairs around the pool. The chairs scraped against the concrete surface as she sorted them. She moved with an efficiency learned by people who have a lot to do and little time.

I had not spoken to her in nearly a week. With her head tilted in concentration, her fine dark hair swayed when she moved. In form-fitting off-white pants and a turquoise sleeveless top, her beauty would compete with the caldera for first prize. I stopped to say hello.

"Morning," I said, breathing heavily from climbing the stairwell two steps at a time.

Selene startled, her thoughts gathering from far away. She stood straight to take me in. Her eyes scanned me from top to bottom then her shoulders drew back, and I recalled the distant and cold manner in which she had checked me in on the first day.

"Oh, Mr. Robbins. It's nice to see you are able to exercise in the morning after your nighttime activities."

What the heck was she talking about?

She turned for another chair. "Julian told me you have found a young woman, and the three of you are now touring the island."

"You're supposed to call me Joe. And yeah, Julian's been great. Yesterday, he took us for lunch at a local farm in the south. They grow much of their own produce."

She stood and faced me again, her lips in a tight frown, and her eyes sparkling with fire. "I have forbidden him from taking you to the nude beaches."

"What?"

Nude beach? The conversation got stranger by the minute. I felt like an ant on a carpet who's just heard the vacuum cleaner.

"You are now stealing from the baby bed. Correct?"

Huh? Baby bed? Oh, jeez, the clichés never translated well.

"No, it's not like that."

"No?" She rocked her head from side to side in the universal way women have of calling men idiots without saying the words. "I see. It is she, the young college girl. She has a fantasy for daddies."

Already warm from my workout, my chest grew hot now, and the heat flushed my face.

"Now that's not right," I said.

"It is always like this with you Americans. You meet someone and hop into bed."

"Are you jealous?"

Her head snapped to me, and she muttered a few words in Greek that I guessed were not in the hotelier training manual.

"Look. We're not sleeping together," I said. "She's in the spare room. And besides, it's not your business if we were. She's twenty-five. Okay? What's the age of consent in Greece?"

Selene was puzzled by my last question. I let it go, opting to take my leave after having the last word. I reached the door to my suite and glanced back. She stood studying the chairs, as if not able to recollect which one to move next.

Chapter 14

THAT NIGHT, THE THREE of us went on a sunset cruise that departed from the old port in Fira in the middle of the afternoon. While riding the funicular cable car to the dock, we watched the donkeys ferrying passengers on the switchbacks of the hill.

We arrived at the bottom twenty minutes early for the cruise and wandered along the dockside. Shuttles from cruise ships pulled up to disgorge noisy passengers heading out for a night of fun. The air carried mixed scents of running boat engines and the sea. Annie and Julian stopped to flip through cards in a shop. A luxury yacht—sixty feet or more—was secured to the dock, and I strolled closer to admire its form. The white hull gleamed in the sun, and a lounging area at the stern made for relaxed sunbathing. A large chair in the middle was rigged for fishing with a heavy rod holder. On the opposite side of the boat, two rods and a gaff were mounted under the rail. The captain's wheel and instruments were on the right side of an open cabin, and a door on the left led to the living quarters below.

A giant of a man stood at the stern and cleaned his fingernails with a fishing knife. Another man climbed the steps from below and sauntered onto the deck. He was perhaps sixty but in good physical condition. In black pants and a white shirt with the sleeves rolled up, he wore his graying hair cut short all the way around his head. He noticed me and immediately smiled, perhaps recognizing me as a tourist.

"Good evening, sir," he said.

I nodded. "You have a beautiful yacht."

"Thank you. Spiro does an excellent job of maintaining it. Don't you, Spiro?"

Spiro grunted, and I guessed that he didn't speak English.

"Do you catch game fish in the Aegean?" I said.

He shook head. "Sadly, no. They are there to be sure, if only I could find the time to steal them from the sea, but alas, I work too much."

"It's a global illness," I said. "You have to learn to be lazy to enjoy life."

He chuckled, and two more men climbed up from the galley.

The first one could have been the yacht owner's twin but for thirty years of difference in age, and I guessed that they were father and son.

I had seen the next man at the side of the road on my first day in Santorini. His name was Markos, and I had bruised his ego in a scuffle.

This must be the Bakas family with their paid help: Markos and the giant named Spiro.

Markos recognized me, walked to the rail, and leaned against the open edge of the wheelhouse with a cruel smile on his lips. He spat, and the spittle landed on the concrete dock a few feet from me.

The yacht owner—who I now assumed was Theo Bakas— scowled when Markos spat, and he strode to the gunwale.

"Do you two know each other?"

Behind Theo, his son Dorian said something quickly in Greek, and Theo laughed.

Markos bristled, and Theo reached across to shake my hand.

"I am Theo Bakas, and you are the man who taught Markos a lesson in manners. Right?"

He had a solid warm grip.

"Joe Robbins."

"You are staying at my friend Giorgos's hotel. We must meet for a drink, you and Giorgos and me. How long are you staying?"

"Another month or so."

"Excellent! I'll get in touch with Giorgos. We'll arrange it."

At that moment, Annie and Julian arrived. Julian hung back from the boat, perhaps nervous to be in close proximity to a powerful Santorini family.

Theo smiled at the boy and nodded at Annie. I made introductions, and Theo shook Annie's hand and waved at Julian.

Off to the side, Markos's smile of cruelty returned. Annie wore a sundress with a low neckline, and his eyes devoured her body from her breasts down to her waist and rounded hips. She noticed him staring and looked away.

He was six feet from me. I could get there in two strides. I'd grab him by the elbow, haul him overboard, and beat him senseless on the dock.

"Joe," she said, "it's time for the cruise."

"Yeah, time for the cruise."

I caught Markos's eye and made sure he could read my emotions. If Theo hadn't been standing there, Markos might have spat on the dock again.

I exchanged parting words with Theo, he promised to connect with Giorgos, and we made our way to the sunset cruise.

We boarded a two-masted sailing vessel with fifty other guests. It stopped at a beach on Nea Kameni—the active volcano—where we swam in waters warmed by natural hot springs. For dinner, they wined and dined us with traditional Greek food and beverages. Then the crew performed folk music and dances. By that time, the guests were liquored up enough to join in, and we held hands and tried to follow the leader's instructions, dancing badly in an extended line that wound around the ship. The sun began to set, and the guests—now sated with food and drink—sat back to enjoy the magnificent view. Julian had found some American high school kids to charm and stayed with them. The ship glided on still waters near Ammoudi Bay, where Annie and I had dined several times.

We sat on a bench on the upper deck with a mesmerizing view of the sunset. Annie leaned into my side, and I put my arm around her. We gazed at the endless sea, and her body warmed mine. It was awfully close to a romantic gesture, but I didn't say anything to stop her. Close friends might have sat the same way without a trace of sexual tension. I told myself it was only a passing moment.

Chapter 15

THE NEXT MORNING, after finishing my workout, I ran into Giorgos outside the lobby. He mentioned that Theo Bakas had called. Giorgos was headed to Athens for the day on business and promised to arrange a meetup for the three of us upon his return. Then he asked about the profitability analysis. I confessed that I hadn't worked on it in over a week.

"Ah, yes," he nodded, and a smile spread across his lips. "Selene told me about this distraction. Is it your niece or a younger cousin? It's hard to keep track."

I mumbled an apology and promised to get back to the project that day.

"That would be splendid," he said with a smirk. "Of course, only if you're not too busy getting reacquainted with your family friend."

He laughed and turned away to ascend the stairs to the top of the cliff.

* * *

UPON HEARING THAT I HAD TO WORK, Annie took a sketchbook she had recently purchased and set out on the trail to Oia.

In my last work session, I had narrowed Giorgos's profit problem to the revenue side of the equation: year-to-date, Giorgos had sold fewer room nights than in the prior year. I had ruled out pricing, distribution, and quality of service as root causes of the shortfall. The problem lay hidden in some other force that drove the rate of occupancy. But how could I detect that force? I struggled to define the best next step.

My mentor at Liberty Air—my first corporate employer—had a saying: When you can't figure out the problem, go back to the cash.

I pulled up the revenue management reports from Boutique HMS and cut the data by type of payment: credit cards, debit cards, corporate accounts, and cash. While credit and debit cards drove a large majority of the settlements, each month, between five and ten percent of tourists paid their bill in cash. They would use a credit card to reserve the room, but when they checked out, they switched to pay with traveler's checks or regular old cash. Perhaps they budgeted their vacation spending that way, unaware that they were dinosaurs in a world rushing toward settling transactions via chips embedded under the skin.

At the Liakáda, total room nights settled with credit or debit cards had increased two percent year over year, similar to the overall revenue trend reported by Giorgos's competitors. However, cash receipts from hotel guests had fallen by sixty percent.

I didn't understand the details yet, but I was willing to bet I could summarize Giorgos's problem with one word: fraud. Employees who seek to steal from their employers often search for ways to finger the cash without leaving a trace.

I cross-referenced bank cash deposits by day with cash receipts reported in the system. The clumsy way to skim cash was to take it out of the till, but that method was easily discovered; only dumb fraudsters went that route. At the Liakáda, cash bank deposits matched reported cash receipts to the last euro. I'd have to dig deeper.

Next, I looked for a way to cross-reference revenue room nights with room nights on the cost side. The Boutique HMS staffing module tracked rooms cleaned by day. To get a baseline, I compared the prior-year May room nights as reported in the staffing module with those reported in the revenue management report. The two figures were off by only a few room nights, possibly driven by human reporting error in the staffing module. But when I ran the comparison for the current year, the discrepancy grew substantially, a fluorescent orange fraud marker. Someone was eliminating cash room nights and taking the money.

Constantine.

Or Selene, possibly, but I considered her a long shot for the embezzler. Constantine was the systems expert. He generated the weekly management report for the bookkeeper. He prepared the daily cash bank deposit slips.

I searched Boutique HMS's library of help topics and learned about the process for voiding room nights after a customer had already checked in. Not often, but once in a while, a hotel customer would check into a room and then immediately check out without paying because the room didn't meet their expectations. Boutique HMS had built the void-room-night procedure for those purposes. According to the online manual, the system auto-generated a monthly report of nights voided, but I couldn't find any of those reports in the files Constantine had shared with Giorgos.

Hmm.

I had used Giorgos's password to log into the Boutique HMS system, but Giorgos had also given me the password Constantine used for the payroll system. A lot of people neglected to create different passwords for different systems, an unwise practice from an information security perspective. How secure was Constantine? I knew his business email address and tried logging onto his email account using the payroll system password. Turned out, Constantine was as lazy as the next guy.

All of his business files were in the cloud. In the old days, people worked on spreadsheets that they could save to a thumb drive and put in their pocket. But you can't put the cloud in your pocket.

Constantine was well organized. It only took a minute for me to find the voided-room-night reports. The money he had stolen from the current tourist season—totaling sixty-five hundred euro—equaled four percent of revenue and explained Giorgos's profit shortfall.

I had already broken into Constantine's business account—a legal act in Texas when acting on behalf of the business owner—so I might as well snoop around. He had loaded a few personal files onto his business drive: photos from a trip he took to Paris and some worksheets unrelated to the Liakáda. A folder name caught my eye: Wastewater Project.

Wait a minute. Giorgos had said Constantine did work for other businesses to make extra money. Did he freelance for the Bakas family? Giorgos was friends with Theo Bakas; perhaps he had put the two of them together.

Did I dare to dive into the Bakas family business? Something about the wastewater project had struck me wrong from the start. They could never lay all those pipelines before the next tourist season.

I had decided not to dig any further when Annie came in. She had run into Constantine outside the lobby, and he had invited us to join him and some friends that night for drinks at a club in Fira. Interesting timing.

Should I call Giorgos to report my findings right away? Or should I wait until the morning, see if I learned anything useful at the club? I decided to wait. With my recent discoveries, I would see Constantine in a different light. Witty and engaging for sure, but like many others, when you blinked away the sparkle, you found a darker side.

Chapter 16

OF ALL THE POSSIBLE names in the world, the club was called Rick's Café Américain. Annie and I ate dinner first and ambled in around eleven. The club had all the right trimmings: tropical plants, ceiling fans, live music with a piano player, even a separate casino room. We found Constantine and his three friends partying at a table with bottle service. He was decked out for fun in nice slacks, a Hawaiian shirt, and his golden slippers.

He signaled a waitress to make us drinks with the high-end vodka. We had driven from Imerovigli, and as the designated driver, I had a convenient excuse to beg off the hard stuff. I ordered a light beer. Good thing. Annie went for a fancy drink, and the bottle waitress had a heavy hand.

Constantine introduced us to his three buddies, and we tried chatting, but the big band music was loud, and his friends were seated on the other side of the table, so we soon clustered into two groups.

I glanced around the club. Nice place. The crowd was affluent. Annie had worn the sexiest outfit she'd packed, a spaghetti-string shiny top over tight-fitting faux leather pants. She stood out as younger than most others in the club; the college kids were on Mykonos or one of the other binge-worthy destinations. In jeans and a polo shirt, I felt underdressed.

For some reason, Annie decided it was the night to party— maybe she tried to compensate for her youth, or maybe she sought to counterbalance my under-consumption, or maybe she had another reason. In any case, she downed her first vodka and then switched to something Constantine recommended. I slowly nursed my first beer.

The conversation wandered around. We discussed the movie *Casablanca*—Constantine and Annie were huge fans—then moved on to other films, Hollywood, celebrities, and fashion. After Annie blew through her third and fourth drink, she became a sloppy drunk. Constantine was no better. He put his arm around her, and at one point, we all came into a group hug. After the hug, Annie casually rested her hand on my leg. She gave my thigh a squeeze.

Hmm. *That didn't feel platonic.*

The topic evolved into future plans. After graduation, Annie would look for a job. I intended to maintain the status quo: consulting in Austin and trying to be a good father. But Constantine had his dream.

"I'm moving to Paris in the fall and will stay for good this time."

"Paris!" exclaimed Annie. "Oh, I love Paris. Can I come to visit?"

"Absolutely, you must." Constantine gazed at me, his eyes sparkling and clear. He wasn't as drunk as I thought. "I'm going to open a retail shop in the premier arrondissement."

When we'd first spoken of his dream, it was a distant aspiration, one that required seed money he needed to save. Now, for some reason, he'd decided to advance the timetable. How much would it cost to open a retail shop in Paris?

It would take a hefty pile for sure: lease deposit and first month's rent, the construction cost for building out the space, inventory, hiring costs, furnishings, back office systems and equipment, utilities, and on and on.

He must have read puzzlement on my face, for he said, "Yes, I have accelerated my plan, even retained a broker to help me search for a good location. I'm putting together artwork for branding and displays, and I've reached out to boutique designers who would kill to display their lineups in Paris."

In her inebriation, Annie showered him with unrestrained adjectives: marvelous, brilliant, delightful. She rested her hand on my shoulder. "Isn't that wonderful, Joe?"

"Super," I said, staring at Constantine. "Fantastic. Do you have your financing lined up?"

He nodded fiercely. "Yes, I have an uncle in Athens who visited last week. He has boatsful of money and loves my business plan." Constantine leaned in. "Honestly, I think my aunt influenced his decision. She loves Paris too."

I didn't believe it from the instant his words reached my ears. Rich uncles don't materialize like rabbits from a hat. Constantine had come into another source of money. His fraud scheme at Liakáda Suites would net him fifteen to twenty thousand euros by the end of the season, far short of the capital he'd need to open a clothing shop.

Annie praised the unseen uncle's familial love and keen business instincts. Constantine ordered shots of ouzo for the table. Everyone else cheered and threw theirs back. I pretended to drink mine but then let it slip from my mouth back into the glass.

No one noticed me push it off to the side. The licorice flavor lingered on my tongue.

After another hour, it was obvious I needed to get Annie out of there. My second beer was still half full.

On the way to the car, she was unsteady, and I held my arm around her for support. Her fingers skimmed the muscles in my chest. In the car, she tried to rub my leg, but with me having to shift gears, it didn't work, and she settled for feeling the back of my neck.

"Joe?" she said in a dreamy voice.

"Yes, Annie."

"I've been thinking."

"Uh huh."

"You're a man, and I'm a woman."

Jeez. Where was she headed with this? We had a good thing going as friends. Of course, nature being what it was, as a man and woman spending a lot of time together, some consideration of intimacy inevitably surfaced. I wasn't immune to those sensations. I had noticed Annie lounging in her skimpy bathing suit poolside, seen her coming out of the bathroom in nothing more than panties and a bra. But I'd screwed up enough times in my life by then that I tried to make decisions using the big head.

Fortunately, while waiting for me to respond, she drifted off. Her hand fell from my neck and rested in her lap. She woke when we arrived at the Liakáda and got out of the car without help. We climbed down the stairs to the suite, and I opened the door. Once inside, I turned toward her. She stood four feet away, staring at me with a strange look on her face, not drunk but not sober either.

"What?" I said.

"You can have me if you want."

Have her? Where did that come from? I stood a little taller and took a half step back.

Using both hands, she pulled her top off in one movement and threw it on the floor. Then she turned one leg to the side—a pretend seductress in her tight leather pants and bra.

"Everyone already thinks we're doing it," she said.

"Who everyone?"

"Selene. The maids. Even Constantine. He said something tonight. Called you a . . . I can't remember the Greek word, but essentially, he called you a dirty old man."

"It doesn't matter what people say. It only matters what we do."

"Why don't you want me? Aren't I pretty enough?"

The whole thing struck me as wrong. Like she felt guilty, or that she owed me something for picking up the room, which made me sick to my stomach.

"You're attractive, Annie. No question. That's not it."

"You think I'm too young."

"You're not too young, just too young for me."

Her shoulders slumped, and I felt like going to her, holding her to make her feel better, but I didn't trust myself. Truthfully, I found her attractive standing there in her tight pants and bra. All that skin and the curve of her breasts started certain nerves tingling that I found hard to ignore.

"Well," she said, "if we're not going to screw, I'll get ready for bed."

"Good idea. You need some sleep."

"Shove it, Robbins."

After she closed the bathroom door, I went into my room and sat on the bed.

Damned if you do. Damned if you don't.

Maybe hers was an alcohol-infused performance. Something she'd regret in the morning, or perhaps not even remember. Yeah. I hoped so.

Carved out of rock like the rest of the apartment, my room had a domed ceiling and enough space for a queen-size bed, a side table, and a small chair, almost claustrophobic with the door closed but big enough for me to do some work.

I opened my laptop and signed into Constantine's cloud-based drive.

His newfound and suspect fortune had piqued my curiosity about his work for the Bakas family on the wastewater project.

The folder contained three files. The first was labeled "WW Budget - First Draft" and was a spreadsheet prepared more than a year earlier by an engineering firm based in Athens. The creator—someone named Zoe Moustakas—knew a lot about these types of projects. Moustakas had built detailed worksheets for different phases. For each step, she had included timeline data and cost estimates that tied back to the overall summary plan. The cost figures provided detailed estimates for materials, labor, land, equipment rentals, and other supplies.

The second file was labeled "WW Project Plan - High Level." I had seen these kinds of layouts before. They were auto-generated by project planning software packages to provide easy-to-consume information for management. I scanned the timetable for the high-level deliverables. By the current date, construction of the processing plant should have been fifty percent complete. Based on my observation, they were still working on the foundation. Trenching and the laying of pipe from Fira to the plant should have been thirty percent complete. In all the times I had driven around with Julian, I had yet to see any trench construction underway. The project was seriously behind schedule.

The third file was meant to reconcile actual costs with planned expenses during each phase of the project. Each stage had rows for costs by category of supplier. For the design phase, the actual costs were in line with the planned costs. The bulk of this spending went to the engineering and project management firm that had created detailed plans for the project. But after the initial phase, the spreadsheet had not been used to record any actual costs.

A separate worksheet in the third file recorded receipts from the government of the special tax assessed to Santorini hotels and restaurants. These entries were current, and the receipts had come in close to the initial projections. To date, ten million euros had been collected.

The final worksheet in the third file contained a simple record of payments made on the project to date. This worksheet did not reflect the refined design skills Zoe Moustakas had employed when constructing the other files. For example, the column and row headings were spelled using all lowercase letters, a style Constantine used for the hotel business. The worksheet contained three columns for each payment: date, amount, and supplier. The numbers recorded payments for the engineering company's work, a few miscellaneous construction invoices, and seven payments to a company called Santorini Management that totaled over four million euros to date.

I whistled.

The payments to other vendors totaled less than one million euros. No construction management company could justify such high overhead charges on a project barely off the ground. Unless the management company was a scam designed to skim monies from a municipal project. Organized crime was famous for this kind of scheme, but they knew how to do it in a way that auditors found hard to trace. In contrast, amateurs of the first order were at work here, people who knew little or nothing about construction or project management or accounting. And those amateurs had invited Constantine into the back office.

It was nearly four o'clock, and my nerves needed steadying, so I poured a Jack Daniels neat. Outside, the three-quarter moon slid toward the western horizon.

I would call Giorgos in the morning and start with a summary update: Greed was alive and well in Santorini, and Constantine was buried in the muck from his slippers to his nose.

Chapter 17

IN THE MORNING, Annie slept off the booze, and I went for a run. Then I called Giorgos from the patio overlooking the caldera. I had much to tell him and preferred to do it face to face. He would return from Athens at noon and suggested a late lunch at his condo in Fira.

Inside the suite, Annie was taking a shower, and I went into my bedroom to check my email. Chandler and Callie had sent a note with a link to photos, and I spent ten minutes writing a response.

When I came out, the door to Annie's room was wide open. She stood with a towel wrapped around her waist and a bra in her hand. Noticing me, her first reaction was to cover herself with her arms. She had dried her hair with a towel, and damp blond curls hung about her shoulders. She stared at me for a long moment, and then dropped her arms. Her breasts were firm and white against the dark of her tan. My heart bounced, and my fingers twitched with the urge to touch her. In two long strides I could have her in my arms. But I hurried out the door, sat in one of the chairs by the pool, and waited for her.

What would I say? When had I last turned down a woman in a similar situation? Ever?

She took her time, perhaps wrestling with multiple emotions: embarrassment, anger, and regret. Damn. The last thing I wanted to do was hurt Annie. I had thought we still had an understanding. I knew where I stood. Hands off. Graduate school was a long time ago for me. Too long. But sometimes understandings have a way of wandering around until the communication is no longer clear.

When she did come out, she sat in the next chair. From her appearance, I wouldn't have known anything had happened. She had dried her hair and put on shorts, a casual shirt, and running shoes. Dark glasses protected her eyes from the sun.

"I'm confused," she said.

"Same here."

"Sorry for the peep show."

"No problem. You have lovely breasts. It's not a question of physical beauty."

She gestured toward the blue caldera. "This is a scene from the movies, too gorgeous to comprehend. I thought we could take it to the next level, like, try friends with benefits."

I shook my head. "That stuff only works in rom-coms."

"I'm confused," she repeated, then lifted her phone. "Matt texted me. He wants to meet up and talk it out."

"Matt? I thought he was long gone. In Madrid or Munich by now."

"He's in Crete. I'm guessing here, but he may have had a fling with an undergrad. Now he's begging me to come back."

My pulse rate jumped. After the way he treated her? "You don't want to do that."

"Don't tell me what I want to do."

"If it's a question of money, I can lend you some."

"Stop giving me money!" She stood so abruptly the chair fell over. Then she stomped back toward the room.

"Annie," I cried to her back. "Let's keep talking."

But she was done talking. Oh, jeez. I sat for ten minutes, replaying the conversation, trying to sort out where I'd gone wrong.

She surprised me by coming out ready to leave, with her backpack zipped closed and strapped on.

I held my hands out in disbelief. "What are you doing?"

"I need space and time," she said. "I'll be in touch." She moved toward the stairwell that led to the walkway to Fira.

"You don't have to leave," I said.

She didn't say another word. Walking away, she held a hand over her shoulder and waved goodbye by flapping her fingers.

I stood at the top of the stairs and watched her go. "Text me that you're okay," I said like a hovering parent to a teenager headed out for the night.

What else could I do? That stubborn, taunting, delightful child-woman would drive me nuts.

Where would she go? I had paid for most of our incidentals, so she still had some money. If Matt truly was on Crete, she could get there by ferry. Or she could go to Athens and arrange to fly home. Or, as I hoped, she might chill in Fira for a couple hours. After cooling off a bit, she would agree to talk things through so we could remain friends.

Chapter 18

GIORGOS HAD A SMALL but well-appointed second-floor condo a few blocks from the bustle of Fira. We sat on a large balcony overlooking a lush courtyard. Bees hovered around the bougainvillea vines that lined the yard below. A faint breeze carried a sweet fragrance from the flowers in the balcony planters.

His housekeeper served us fish sandwiches accompanied by potato chips. She had cooked the tuna medium and spread a tangy curry sauce on the bread. The chips may have been for my benefit.

In a short-sleeved buttoned shirt, Giorgos sat back with his arms folded over his big belly and frowned as I provided details of Constantine's fraud scheme. He said he wished I had found some other problem, a fault with operations or distribution.

"I can understand the temptation," he said. "Everyone wants a few more euros than he has now, but I wish he'd come to me directly."

Giorgos had known Constantine since he was a small boy and also knew his family. Then Giorgos grew quiet, occasionally twiddling his thumbs, perhaps considering the big question. Should he report the fraud to the police or not? If he did, Constantine would likely go to jail, an outcome certain to be unpopular with Constantine's family and perhaps other locals. The lighter course would be for Giorgos to fire Constantine and demand the return of his money. He might have leaned that way, but that alternative struck me as untenable given the bigger issue at hand.

"There's more," I said.

His demeanor further changed when I explained my discoveries related to the wastewater project. First, his eyebrows scrunched so far I could scarcely see his eyes. Then he began chewing the inside corner of his mouth. He drummed his fingers on the armrest. Finally, he said in a voice barely under control, "Are you certain?"

"I know the payments were recorded in Constantine's spreadsheet."

Giorgos slammed the table. "This is Dorian Bakas's work! Damn him!" He held his hand out in rage, his fingers like claws. "I'll have his balls myself."

"Don't you think his father is probably directing the whole thing?"

"No. No. Theo is smart. This is stupid. Theo wanted us to appoint his son as the managing partner of the development company to build the project. We agreed, under the condition that Theo would monitor the situation closely. He has failed to do that, and I will hold him accountable."

"We should report this to the police. Right?"

Giorgos raised his eyebrows as if he hadn't considered that possibility. "Perhaps. That course is inconsistent with what you called Santorini style, but if the situation is not fixed—if the Bakas family does not return the money—Dorian will have to go to prison. The hoteliers and restaurant owners will demand it."

It made me uneasy. I could live with slapping Constantine's wrist for the hotel theft. It was Giorgos's hotel and his money. But ignoring the wastewater fraud scheme smelled like day-old fish.

Giorgos put his hands up. "I can see you have concerns. Don't worry. I'll take care of it. Your work is done."

"Are you sure? This is a big deal. In the States, we put people in small rooms for years when they steal from the public."

He rocked his head from side to side. "Yes, but this is not the U.S. We'll handle it our way."

"All right." I gave up. When in Santorini, and so forth.

"How is your sandwich?" he asked.

"It's good."

"The tuna is okay?"

"Excellent. Best ever."

"Have a little more wine."

"Sure. Why not?"

Chapter 19

AFTER THE MEETING with Giorgos, I went in search of Annie. It was too soon to text her. We had spent every day together for well over a week, and she needed time on her own to acquire a fresh perspective. If she was already on a ferry to Crete or Athens, I would likely never see her again. If she had decided to stick around, more time worked in my favor.

Still, I couldn't resist searching for her all over Fira.

Budget hotels lined the side streets on the east side of the main road through town. Signs announced rooms for fifty euros. The backpacker crowd stayed there. I stopped a few women on the sidewalk and showed them a picture of Annie on my phone. Had they seen her? No luck.

Back in the busy side of town, I wandered through the streets of the tourist section until I got lost, then kept going until I found my way again. I strolled through a hundred shops and restaurants and bars. More than once, I cruised by the sidewalk café where we had first met. I stood at the top of the hill and stared at the dockside, trying to pick out a girl that might be Annie. After several hours, I knew the streets of Fira well but had found no trace of her.

Maybe she had gone back to the room. As I drove the winding road to Imerovigli, my stomach rolled. She wasn't in the room. Finally, I texted her and waited. After ten minutes, I hiked into the village for a gyro and a salad. I went to bed around eleven and lay with my eyes open and my ears hoping for the text ding from my phone.

There was no reason to worry about her. At the age of twenty-five, she could line up the pros and cons and make smart decisions. Annie knew her own mind. If I couldn't see things her way, no problem—she would move on.

Chapter 20

I WOKE EARLY AND HIKED to Fira and back, stopping periodically to observe the caldera in the quiet morning light. An old man who sold souvenir pins on the walkway had arrived early to erect his easels and prepare for business. Countless days in the sun had turned his skin a dark brown. Gray hair poked out from the edges of his cap. He always set up shop at the same turn on the path, and we recognized each other.

He nodded, and I said, "Hello."

"Where is your friend today?" he asked, meaning Annie. She had always stopped to consider his buttons. He had joked with her, asked her why such a pretty woman was not already married.

"She has gone to another island," I said.

"You are sad, yes? Sad that she has gone away."

I shrugged.

"Don't worry. She will come back. Each time she touches the same buttons, and I know she will return to buy them."

I did not share the old man's faith. Who would go out of their way to buy souvenir buttons? On the way back to Imerovigli,

I stared at the path, scarcely noticing the view. My feet were well acquainted with the crooked turns and rough spots.

At the Liakáda, I trudged up the stairs to my level and came upon a curious sight on the patio. The two maids from my hotel often shared an early breakfast with several maids from nearby properties. They would cluster on the patio to share news and eat before beginning the day's work. But on that morning, they stood together and stared at Skaros Rock, the towering peninsula I had climbed weeks ago. One of the women asked a question, and the others shook their heads.

Christina—the maid who cleaned my room every day—waved me over. An energetic woman not an inch over five feet, Christina always wore a cheerful expression, but today, worry lines creased her brow.

"Mr. Robbins," she said, pointing. "There is something on Skaros. Do you see it?"

My eyes scanned the rocky surface of the tower for several seconds before I noticed a white object that stood out against the gray of the shale-like incline a third of the way down from the peak. At that distance, I couldn't discern the object's nature. At one edge, the white material seemed to move as if flapping in the breeze—a trash bag perhaps, filled with something heavy enough to anchor it in place.

"Can you get your glasses?" said Christina, "that you use to see far away?" She held curled hands to her eyes to mimic the lenses of my binoculars.

I retrieved the binoculars from my room and trained them on the object.

My heart rate accelerated like a race car off the starting line. It was a human being. Not moving. Probably dead.

I took a deep breath and exhaled slowly, my mind replaying the climactic scene of someone's life. He or she had jumped from the peak, landed on the rocks, and tumbled down the incline another fifty yards. I couldn't see a head; perhaps it lay pinned awkwardly beneath the body. The white shirt and pants were torn, shredded by the rocks as the body rolled. A piece of the shirt hung loose and moved gently in the wind. Patches of exposed skin on the back and shoulders displayed the cruel gashes and abrasions inflicted by the rocks.

One hand reached out from beneath the body in an unnatural way as if the force of the fall had ripped the arm from the shoulder. The two legs were intact with the knees bent and the feet in full view. One foot was bare, but the other had miraculously retained its shoe. Even at that distance, I could see it clearly: a shiny golden slipper.

I closed my eyes behind the binoculars. A low moan escaped my throat.

Two nights earlier, we had toasted his upcoming adventure in Paris. I had pretended to drink the ouzo, plotting even then to crawl through his files until I knew all his secrets.

He had been happy.

"What is it?" asked Christina.

My shoulders sank, and I lowered the binoculars.

I eyed Christina and the other maids. They could read from my expression that I had bad news. Perhaps I should have considered the situation more carefully, the closeness of the community, the cheerfulness he had brought to the neighborhood, greeting everyone with a warm smile and a kind word, but after glancing at each of the maids briefly, I said the only words that came to mind.

"It's Constantine."

Christina gasped, brought her hand to her mouth, and gaped at Skaros. Some of the maids spoke only a little English, but they had all understood me. One of them shrieked and covered her face. Another asked me if I was sure. I nodded. They chattered busily in Greek, absorbing the news, and then they cried, all of them, the commencement of communal grieving.

Within five minutes, over a dozen people had gathered and were in varying states of shock. The word would spread like wildfire. Soon, curious boys would cross the isthmus for a closer look.

I pulled out my cell and called Captain Veggos. After I explained that Constantine lay dead on the incline, Veggos said nothing at first. What was he thinking? Perhaps he found it suspicious that I had now discovered *two* bodies on Santorini. Finally, he promised that uniformed policemen would arrive within ten minutes.

The next four hours were a bit of a circus. Over a thousand people came to stand on the walkway and stairwells of the cliffside to watch the spectacle of the police trying to remove the body. The onlookers took pictures with their phones and undoubtedly posted the sensational news on social media. Two brave policemen tried traversing the steep incline of loose rock to reach Constantine. They made it twenty feet and then realized they were in grave danger of slipping and rolling down the hill. The police then decided to try it from below. A patrol boat pulled up to where the rock plunged into the sea, and two experienced climbers got out. They had rope and some sort of anchoring device that gave them stability for the climb. Eventually, they reached the corpse and hauled a stretcher up from the boat. Within an hour, they had loaded him and motored away, ending the drama.

Throughout the show, I caught glimpses of the captain directing operations and talking on his cell phone. He sent officers out to interview locals in the crowd. No one came to interview me. I figured the captain would do that himself.

As I waited, my mind wrestled with the question of how Constantine had wound up on that incline. My first thought was suicide. The day we met, he had described Skaros Rock as a prime spot from which to take one's final step. Having glanced over the edge, I had to agree.

So, what was his motive? Simple. After meeting with me, Giorgos had undoubtedly fired Constantine and demanded the return of his money. Giorgos may have confronted him with the wastewater scam. In any case, Constantine's vision of opening a shop on Rue Saint Honoré had vanished in a few short minutes. It can be hard to let go of a dream. Like countless sufferers before him, Constantine had opted to end the pain quickly.

Hmm. Maybe. That was one scenario. On the other hand, when I asked if he had scaled the peak himself, Constantine said he had not and never would due to his fear of heights. So why did he? There were easier ways to off oneself.

Giorgos had not seemed in a hurry to confront Constantine with the hotel fraud. It was only a few thousand euros. But he'd been furious about the wastewater project, perhaps mad enough to demand an immediate audience with Theo Bakas.

Could that conversation have had something to do with Constantine lying on the side of the hill? Perhaps Giorgos had spoken to both Constantine and Theo.

I had many theories and no facts, and it wasn't my deal anyway.

But my musings convinced me to make one decision: Despite Giorgos's desire to handle things Santorini style, when the captain arrived, I would tell him everything I knew.

Chapter 21

VEGGOS CLIMBED TO THE PATIO at noon. The sun had already heated the day, and perspiration shone on his brow. I offered him ice water, which he gratefully accepted. After drinking half the glass, he asked if I knew of any reason for Constantine to commit suicide.

"Perhaps," I said. "Was it suicide?"

"I don't know. It's early. The body is a mess. We'll know more after the autopsy. But in the meantime, we ask questions."

I described the profitability project I had conducted for Giorgos. As my story unfolded, Veggos began to nod, perhaps thinking the suicide scenario had come into focus.

"Yes," he said, "this would be a cause of great shame in the community, to steal from someone who has helped you. And there is the issue of the lost dream. Perhaps it makes sense."

Then I told him about the wastewater project. He stiffened in the chair, and his eyes widened. Then he shook his head and breathed loudly through his nose.

"Oh, this is bad. You discussed this with Giorgos?"

I nodded.

"This is bad. I don't know how to . . . Let me think." He pulled his chin, rubbed his hand over his whole face, and pulled his chin some more.

"I have to go to Athens," he said.

"Why?"

"You need to be careful. Don't wander around at night. Stay close to your hotel."

"What are you talking about?"

He glanced over both shoulders to make sure no one could hear us.

"I told you before I am not from Santorini. I don't know who I can trust. I have two men on my team that might be solid, but even them . . . I have to talk to some officials with the federal police, people I know, to get advice."

Then he gazed out to the peninsula.

"I have never been up Skaros Rock," he said, "but I am told it is a difficult climb, that no one could carry another person to the top."

"I've been to the peak," I said. "I could do it. It wouldn't be easy, but if the person were unconscious, say, or already dead, it could be done."

He nodded. "Thank you. Your information will help us in the investigation."

I expected him to stand and shake hands, but he lingered. His eyes softened, and then he looked away.

"What is it?" I said.

"I have something to tell you, something difficult. It was strange that you called when you did today, because I was about to call you."

My heart began to race. I held my breath. "Why?"

"Do you remember the story I told you of the man on the cruise ship who jumped overboard?"

"Sure. The man who killed Crystal."

"Apparently, he did not kill Ms. Reiter."

"He didn't?"

"Interpol called yesterday. In the U.S., the local police from the town where the man lived recently found the body of a missing woman. They believe she was killed by the man on the cruise ship."

My mind scurried to stay with Veggos. The man on the ship had babbled to a bartender about murder and rape and having to pay the price.

"I sent an officer to the hotel gift shop to question the clerk again. She is no longer sure the man from the cruise ship bought flowers that day. Apparently, another man buys flowers from her every week, and she has grown confused."

"That's insane. You're saying Crystal's murderer is at large."

"Yes. We must reopen the investigation."

I blinked several times as I sorted through his revelation. The muscles in my neck grew tense, and I ground my teeth. At the side of the luxury yacht, Markos had devoured Annie's body with his eyes. He had smiled the smile of the schoolboy who gets away with everything.

Captain Veggos pointed at me. "Don't do anything stupid."

"It's Markos," I said. "I can feel it. It's him."

"We have no evidence of that. Don't do anything until I return from Athens. I'll reach out to you then. In the meantime, stay here at the Liakáda."

Chapter 22

I HADN'T EATEN ALL DAY, so I grabbed a shower and climbed the stairs to the village for a sandwich. A quiet had fallen among the pine trees and the walkways. Radios that normally played lively music were silent. People grouped in twos and threes in doorways and spoke in hushed tones. Even the birds refused to sing; apparently, they too mourned the loss of Constantine.

On the way back to my room, I stopped at the lobby to check in with Selene. Seeing me enter, she popped up from behind the desk and rushed toward me. Grabbing my arm, she pulled me farther into the office, then ducked her head outside to check for onlookers. Her eyes were tinged pink as if she had cried earlier, but she moved quickly now. The grief would have to wait.

"Joe, where have you been?" She pushed me toward a chair.

"I went for lunch."

She sat next to me and twisted the rings on her fingers. "Did you see Giorgos?"

"No."

"You must have just missed him. He left minutes ago."

"What's going on? Why are you excited?"

She sat with knees together and head high. Her eyes searched mine as if seeing me for the first time. My stature had risen from obnoxious American to some higher level as yet undefined.

"Giorgos told me about the work you've done for him, how you discovered that Constantine has been stealing."

"Oh."

"Giorgos must have told others, for the rumor has spread. One of the maids already heard it from her cousin."

Had Giorgos told her everything or only the part about the hotel theft?

"People are saying that Constantine was ashamed, that he couldn't stand to face the villagers, and so he took his own life."

"What do you think?"

She made a face like she'd tasted rotten fruit. "This is kaka, this rumor. Bad lies." She gazed out the window in longing, as if she knew that beyond the walkway the stunning view had vanished and she wanted to see it once more.

"I have known Constantine my whole life," she said in a softer voice. "We played together in school. He has faced many crises: death, humiliation, and abuse. He survived them all with his spirit intact. Despite the hatred and fear in others, Constantine always greeted newcomers with an open heart. He loved bright colors and music and dancing. He would never have done this thing. Suicide."

"So you believe he was murdered."

"Yes! And Giorgos does too. He was furious. I have never seen him like this."

"Who does Giorgos think killed Constantine?"

She shook her head. "He wouldn't tell me."

Giorgos must have blamed the Bakas family. I was dying to call him, but not in front of Selene. Perhaps he had met with Theo Bakas the day before and mentioned that I had discovered

Constantine's involvement in the wastewater scheme. Later, Theo had ordered Constantine killed. I remembered the giant I had seen on Bakas's yacht. His name was Spiro, and he had massive arms. Spiro could easily have hauled Constantine to the peak of Skaros Rock.

But that course struck me as extreme. Bakas could have counted on Constantine's silence because of his involvement. Why kill him now?

While I wrestled with the mystery of motive, Selene watched me.

"You *know* something," she said. "You met with the captain on the patio for a long time. Don't tell me. Giorgos told me not to ask. He said you are in danger, and that we must help you."

"Me?"

"Yes. We must leave now. I am to take you to an unoccupied condo in Oia that Giorgos owns."

The course struck me as overly precautious. This wasn't Sicily. I hadn't violated the principle of omertà.

But then I recalled the abrasions on Constantine's body from rolling down the incline. *That* was extreme. I would go along with Giorgos's suggestion. But what about Annie? What if she returned to my suite while I was gone? No. There was little chance of that. I had sent her six or seven texts, and she had ignored them all. She was safe on Crete by now.

"All right," I said. "I'll stay in Giorgos's place for the night."

I told Selene I would grab a few things from my room and be ready to go in ten minutes.

My room was a few steps from the foot of the stairs. At the door, I pulled my passkey from my pocket and heard a footstep behind me.

Two men in casual clothes stood close by: Markos and Dorian Bakas. They must have been waiting for me, perhaps standing behind the large potted plant next to the pool. Dorian held a semiautomatic pistol casually pointed at my midsection.

In spite of the gun, at the sight of Markos, heat rushed to my chest, and my vision grew blurry around the edges. He had murdered Crystal, and I would punish him, beat him senseless and then beat him some more, but the aimed barrel kept my fists in check.

In tight faded jeans, a white T-shirt he wore to show off his weight-lifting muscles, and a pretty-boy smile, Markos resembled a nightmarish version of a young Marlon Brando. His boss wore Italian loafers with no socks, dark pants with a white shirt, and sunglasses.

Dorian smiled and said with an English accent, "Might we have a little talk, please?" He gestured with the handgun. "Inside your room?"

Would he shoot me? On the patio of the hotel? Did he know how to use his weapon? I deemed it too risky to rush them both and waved my passkey to open the door.

We settled into seats, me on the couch, Dorian on an armchair facing away from the door, and Markos on a chair opposite the coffee table from me. A bowl of fruit sat on the table, oranges and apples. The cash I had hidden my first day rested securely in the cushion behind my back. Dorian's full head of hair was wavy and carefully groomed.

He lit a cigarette and searched the table. "No ashtray? And they call this place upscale." He motioned with his head for Markos to find something, and the errand boy returned with a juice glass half filled with water.

Markos sat with his legs spread and his hand in his lap.

What did they want with me? The whole thing smelled of amateur hour, like they had watched too many episodes of *The Sopranos*. If they killed me here, they'd never get away with it. Someone had undoubtedly seen them walking in the area or would see them leaving. The murder of an American is a big deal the world over.

"Let's talk about spreadsheets," said Dorian. "I want to know what you know."

"Nothing. I did a little work for Giorgos."

"That's not what he told my father," said Dorian.

"Is that why you killed Constantine?"

"I have nothing against gays," said Dorian. "I lean that way myself from time to time. But the little thief from Imerovigli tried to blackmail me, wanted three hundred thousand euros to keep his mouth shut. He should have known better."

"Who hauled him up Skaros?" I said, my eyes on Markos. "It wasn't you. Your muscles are all show."

"He had some help," said Dorian.

Spiro, I thought, *the giant on the luxury yacht.* Carrying Constantine to the peak had been small work for him.

Markos said something in Greek, and Dorian chuckled.

"Careful, Joe. Markos is not so good with his fists, but he is skilled with a knife. He said he'd cut off your manhood and stick it in your mouth."

Nice language from the yahoo. I guessed that trading tough-talk jabs would get me nowhere, so I tried appealing to Dorian's common sense.

"You've got nothing to worry about with me," I said. "I'm only a guy on vacation. I couldn't care less what you Greeks do to each other out here in the islands."

"Who did you talk to about the wastewater project?"

"No one, except for Giorgos. He paid me to work on the hotel analysis. When I stumbled onto the management company payments, I felt obligated to tell him about them."

Dorian frowned. The air was thick with smoke.

"It's the truth," I said.

Markos said something else, a short sentence.

Dorian's eyes turned dark. He clenched his jaw, and his cheek muscles bulged. I honestly thought he might shoot me right then, but his cell rang, and after glancing at the screen, he answered the call.

The voice on the other end asked a short, loud question. Dorian answered in a few sentences. The voice said, "No," then went on for a while, louder, more insistent. Dorian lit another cigarette and glanced at Markos. Markos's face turned neutral. I got the impression the voice had authority over Dorian. Dorian said "Okay," and the voice added emphasis to his statement. This happened twice again, and then Dorian rang off in frustration.

I breathed in deeply. It appeared that I might live after all, at least for the moment.

"I want you to take a drive with us," Dorian said, "but first I need the combination to your safe." He shrugged. "I promised Markos."

I gave them the combination. Markos rushed to the safe and returned to his seat waving my two thousand dollars with a bully's smile on his face.

Better make a move soon.

If I got in the car with those two, I'd never make it back to the hotel.

"Let me ask you again," said Dorian. "Who did you talk to about the wastewater payments?"

"I told you the truth. I spoke to no one but Giorgos."

Markos spoke again, louder this time.

"What did he say?" I asked.

"Markos thinks you're lying."

"I don't know what you pay him for, but it's certainly not to think."

Markos rubbed his crotch like he was trying to arouse himself. He spoke a long sentence. I had an idea of his meaning.

"What did he say?" I said.

Dorian dropped his cigarette in the glass and shook his head. "It's better if I don't translate that."

"She wanted it bad," said Markos, meaning Crystal. He stroked his crotch again. "I fucked her and fucked her and fucked her."

A loud click sounded in my head. A mad wave washed over me. I grabbed the nearest object—an orange from the bowl on the table—and threw it at Markos. The orange beaned him on the forehead, and he jerked back in his chair. Dorian had just reached for another cigarette and struggled to aim his pistol. He fired high. In the close cave room, the shot sounded like a cannon. The bullet ricocheted crazily off the walls several times before taking out a lampshade and embedding itself in the couch with an explosion of stuffing.

I jumped toward Dorian, knocked his gun hand up, and ran two steps to get out the door. Bright sunshine blinded me, and I almost tripped lunging down the nearby stairwell. In three bounds I had reached the next level, and I turned right to sprint past the nearest rooms. The door to the second room had been propped open with a trashcan. I ran into the room, nudged the trashcan out of the way, and locked the door. Then I gasped for air, my heart jackhammering in my chest.

Had they seen me come into the room? I had made it there quick, and it must have taken them at least a few seconds to figure out what to do. Someone might have noticed the gunshot. They couldn't afford to stick around after that.

I scanned the room. No one was home. I forced myself to breathe steadily. In. Out. In. Out. My heart began to settle.

Five minutes later, someone knocked. I put my eye to the peephole and was relieved to find a customer of the hotel, an older gentleman with a scowl on his face.

"Jeez," I said, after opening the door. "I'm sorry. I came in a few seconds ago and then realized I was in the wrong room." I hurried out and turned toward the stairs. "I'm ditzy today, can't get anything straight."

The man did not respond, and I trod softly toward the stairs, my eyes darting everywhere, scouting for Dorian and Markos, but they must have scampered. Back at my room, I found Selene.

"What happened here?" she exclaimed after I let her into the room.

I explained as I unzipped the cushion from the sofa and used my pocketknife to slice through the stitches and retrieve my three thousand in cash.

"Dorian Bakas fired a gun at you?"

"I'll tell you everything in the car."

I threw a few things in a day bag and grabbed my laptop, binoculars, and hat.

"I'm ready."

Chapter 23

I HUNCHED IN THE PASSENGER seat of Selene's tiny car and pulled my hat down low. The engine whined when she shifted the gears. As I related my story about the public project fraud and my conversation with Dorian, Selene began to drive faster. The two-lane road from Imerovigli to Oia has many curves. When the tires of her car squealed around a corner, I asked her to drive slower.

The road came to a steep hill. After downshifting, she glanced at me, her eyes aflame.

"They killed Constantine over money!" she spat. "They should pay with their lives."

"I need to call Giorgos."

I reached Giorgos on my cell. He was as angry as Selene.

"This is all Dorian's doing," he shouted. "He'll have to go to prison."

The way he said the words puzzled me. It was as if the proper punishment for Dorian had been an open question until that moment, as if in the context of Santorini style, the wastewater fraud scheme might have been pushed to the side, but *now* that Dorian was implicated in the death of Constantine, his fate was sealed.

"What about Markos?" I said.

"Don't worry about Markos. Theo Bakas will take care of him shortly."

The code of the Santorini network grew stranger by the minute. How connected was Giorgos? Did he know of the public works fraud even before I told him?

"I met with Theo last night," said Giorgos. "He had only learned of Dorian's incompetence in managing the wastewater project a few days ago. He said he'd take care of everything, but he needed some time."

Incompetence. Dorian was not dishonest when he stole from citizens. He was incompetent in how he went about it. Giorgos had a strong command of the English language, and I doubted he had used the word by mistake. It was as if Giorgos expected, or perhaps everyone expected, that Dorian would skim some money from the project, but that he had been greedy, and he'd bungled his oversight of the construction as well.

Until that moment, I had planned to tell Giorgos about my conversation with Captain Veggos and that the captain had gone to Athens for advice, but I held back. I didn't know Giorgos well. I didn't know anyone on the island well. I glanced at Selene. Could I trust her? Was she driving me to Theo Bakas that very moment?

No. Her lips were still drawn tight. Her anger was genuine.

She drove with confidence, her hands tightly gripping the wheel, her strong arms shifting the gears without hesitation, her legs and feet working the clutch, accelerator, and brake pedals smoothly. Her straight dark hair brushed the tops of her shoulders. She wore three silver earrings: a moon, a star, and a medium size hoop. We rolled over a bump, and her body jostled delightfully. In the excitement of the moment, I found her immensely attractive.

Giorgos told me he would reach out to Theo again and that I should wait for his word at the condo in Oia.

Selene and I spoke little for the rest of the way. She parked on a side street and escorted me a few blocks to a two-story residential building that overlooked the promenade. We climbed one flight, and she let me in with a key. The condo was huge, luxuriously decorated, and had a large balcony. We stood outside to take in the view. We were fifteen feet above the promenade at the edge of the cliff. A west wind carried the smell of the sea. Two islands were close by, Thirasia to the right and Nea Kameni in the middle of the caldera. Tourists strolled on the promenade and stopped in shops. Recorded soft rock music drifted over from a restaurant.

Selene inspected the contents of the kitchen and found they lacked some of life's necessities.

"You have wine and coffee but no food. I'll bring dinner around seven o'clock."

"You don't have to do that. There are plenty of places to eat close by."

"Don't go out. The Bakas family have many connections throughout Santorini. They may have spread the word to look for you."

"Perhaps I should go to the police," I said, because I wanted to hear her response.

She shook her head instantly. "No, Theo Bakas also has friends in the police force. Giorgos wants you to wait here, and I agree. You should probably avoid the balcony also. There are many eyes in Oia."

"Okay."

Selene left soon after, and I immediately called the captain. He answered on the third ring, and I filled him in. When I told him Dorian Bakas had tried to kill me, he cursed in Greek.

"What should I do?" I said.

"Stay there. I have no means of assuring your safety, and I believe you can trust Giorgos. He's connected in Santorini, but he's not a criminal."

"When are you coming back?"

"I have two meetings tomorrow mid-day. If those go well, I'll bring federal resources to help clean this mess. In any case, I'll return on the evening ferry."

Thus began the longest twenty-four hours of my life, interrupted only by two pleasant visits from Selene. By the time she brought dinner—a delicious paella with fish, vegetables, and rice—I had sorted the Wi-Fi and music. I played low-key jazz to settle my nerves. She accepted a glass of white wine and kept me company while I ate.

She sat across from me at the white kitchen table, and we had our first real conversation. We talked about kids awhile, comparing our experiences with the challenges, hopes, and fears of raising teenagers. We were both interested in music without having any particular talent in the area. She was a keen follower of the International Songwriting Competition because it exposed her to new music from all over the world: rock from Bulgaria, folk from South Africa, and jazz from Japan. I asked what she liked to do when she wasn't working or taking care of Julian. Like most single mothers, she had little free time. Oddly enough for an islander in the Mediterranean, she said she most missed going to the beach. She loved to relax under an umbrella with a good book to read and the sound of the surf in the background. Afterward, she liked to clean up and dine on fresh seafood at a casual restaurant. Both activities sounded great to me.

At the door to leave, she leaned forward for a hug and gave me a parting peck on the cheek. We had come a long way. Standing there, she touched my hand lightly and let the contact linger.

"Not everyone in Santorini is like the Bakas family. Most of the people who live here are good."

"I'm sure they are," I said. "That's been my experience wherever I go. Most people are good people."

Her gaze lingered, and then she nodded, promised to visit again in the morning, and left.

I poured a second glass of wine and sat on the balcony with the lights out and my chair far enough from the edge that no one could see me from the promenade below. At the horizon, the union of sea and sky glowed orange. Farther away from the sun, the sky turned a bright powder blue. I remained on the balcony long after the wine was gone and the sun had set.

I missed Annie. Why the dickens hadn't she responded to any of my texts? Enough was enough. She had played the spurned woman with hurt feelings for too long. It was time to make up.

And why the hell was I still in Santorini? One reason only: I meant what I said when I told the captain two weeks earlier that I would stay until he caught Crystal's murderer. The vacation had grown bitter in some respects and dangerous in others, but I remained committed to seeing justice served for Crystal's death.

Chapter 24

IN THE MORNING, Selene returned to the condo with a new idea.

"You should leave," she said, after laying out breakfast food on the kitchen table. She had brought pastries and cut fruit. Standing next to the table in a white and blue striped shirt, long dark pants, and high heels, she added, "It's dangerous, and sooner or later the Bakas family will find you here."

"Giorgos said to stay in the condo."

"Yes, but Giorgos does not control you."

"It might be dangerous for me to go to the airport or the ferry terminal."

"Yes, I know, but there are some people I trust. They have boats. They could safely take you to Athens or Crete, or even to Italy."

"I think I'll chance it another day or two."

Her brow wrinkled, and she clasped her hands. "Are you sure?"

I tried a joke. "Why are you so eager for me to leave?"

"I don't *want* you to leave." She cocked her head slightly. "But I don't want you to stay if staying would cause you harm."

"Let me think it over," I said. "I appreciate your concern, but I want to give it one more day."

Selene shrugged. "Okay. I tried. It's your life."

At the door, she gave me another peck on the cheek, and then hurried down the stairs. Over breakfast, I drank two cups of strong coffee and mentally prepared myself for another boring day of waiting to hear from the captain or Giorgos.

* * *

BY TWO O'CLOCK, I had marched a complicated route around the condo at least fifty times. I had organized all the files on my laptop. Periodically, I caught my hands wringing each other and forced them to stop.

After eating a sandwich that Selene had brought, I sat on the balcony, back from the edge. If I couldn't walk through the world, or even see it, at least I could listen to the interactions of people on the promenade below.

My cell rang.

It was Annie. Finally.

"Hey! Annie!"

Silence from the other end, and then a man's voice said, "I'm afraid not."

Was that Matt? No, the voice sounded Greek and familiar, but I couldn't place him. My mind rushed to conclusions. She had gotten into some sort of trouble, perhaps been hurt in an accident. This was the police or the hospital.

"Who is this?"

A heavy sigh came through the earpiece. "We met once on the dockside at the old port. Annie is here with me."

Then I placed him. Theo Bakas, the leader of the local mob, the man who Giorgos counted on to fix everything, had Annie's phone. My heart rate accelerated. I stood and stared at the caldera, not seeing anything.

"Let me talk to her."

"I'm sorry about the incident at your hotel. Sometimes my son complicates matters. I came by last night to apologize, but you had gone. Fortunately, your friend was there."

I clenched the phone. "What do you want?"

"Ha!" he exclaimed. "Just like an American. You must get straight to the point. No time for pleasantries."

I didn't have a handle on Bakas. Giorgos believed he was a reasonable person caught in an unreasonable situation. His son and Markos had gotten out of control, and he needed time to sort things out. But now he had kidnapped Annie, a provocative move by anyone's rules.

"You want to make small talk?" I said. "Go ahead. I'm listening."

He paused. "You've spoiled the moment. Did you discuss the wastewater project with anyone else?"

"No. Giorgos. That's it."

"Why has Captain Veggos made an unscheduled trip to Athens?"

Damn.

"Has he? I wouldn't know why. Maybe he needs help handling two simultaneous murder investigations. Turn Markos in. You'll save him a lot of trouble."

"It's not a bad thought. Markos is a liability."

"Why are you holding Annie?"

"She's my guest. I need insurance. Of course, if you came to me, I could let her go."

"Fine. Where are you? I'll be right over."

Bakas paused to consider that. If he didn't trust me on the question of who I had talked to, how could he trust me with his location? He couldn't.

"You'd better not harm her," I said. "If Markos or any other person hurts her in any way, I will hold you responsible."

"That sounded like a threat."

"It was. Put her on the phone. I need to know she's okay."

The sound went dead. He had put me on mute. After a few more seconds, Annie spoke to me.

"Joe?"

"Are you okay?"

"I'm sorry. I wanted to surprise you."

"Don't worry about that. Are you okay?"

"Y-yes?" she said as if not entirely sure.

"Hang on, Annie. I'm coming for you."

She tried to reply, but her voice was muffled. I imagined someone dragging her from the room.

"Very touching," said Bakas. "You idiot. I've got you on speaker. Now listen. This is the plan. I'm going to give you an address. You meet my associates there at midnight tonight, and we will free the girl."

"Not a chance. Have them meet me in downtown Fira at five o'clock. Bring Annie, and we'll do the exchange there."

Again, he paused. That didn't work either. I could easily sabotage the handoff.

"We are at an impasse," he said. "Maybe I will come to you."

I had to knock the cockiness out of Theo's voice. He would only protect Annie if he feared me.

"You'll never find me," I said.

"This is a small island," he said. "Even the rocks have eyes and ears, and they are all beholden to me."

"If Annie suffers one scratch, one lost button, or a smudge on her clothes, I will find you, and I will kill you."

"So dramatic," he said.

"Others who failed to heed my threats now breathe the sulfuric fumes of hell."

"As you Americans say, talk is cheap."

"Ignore me, and you'll find it damned expensive. I won't go to the police. I'll take care of you Santorini style."

"Tsk, tsk. We will see who finds who."

And then he rang off. My hands shook from tension. I paced the length of the balcony, breathing lungsful of air to calm my mind.

Words alone would not save Annie, or me for that matter. Only action could do that. Theo Bakas had many advantages in this fight, but I had one: Captain Veggos and his federal officers. I called the captain but got his voice mail. Same deal with Giorgos.

I sat on the balcony to think.

Bakas had sounded mighty confident. Had Giorgos told him of my whereabouts? Not likely. They would have come for me already.

The rocks have eyes. What crap—old-world nonsense. I stared at my phone. He had my number now. Maybe Theo would eschew folklore for new technology. If he had a contact at the wireless provider on Santorini, they could track me within a few feet. They could find me, kill me, and do what they chose with Annie. Of course, I could easily disable the signal by turning off my phone.

Or not.

Chapter 25

AFTER COPYING A FEW numbers from my phone, I deleted everything on it. Then I solicited Selene's help with my scheme. I needed a car and a driver, and she lived less than a mile away on the outskirts of Oia. I stashed my stuff in her car and then stopped in a consumer gadget shop to buy a prepaid phone. I loaded the few numbers I needed into the cell and then roamed back and forth on the walkways of Oia for an hour. By then I had a map of the place in my head.

It was another cloudless hot day in Santorini. Soon tourists would begin to gather to capture selfies with the sunset. The prime viewing spot was the Oia Castle ruins above the trail that led to Ammoudi Bay. A rock wall four feet high lined the edge of the promenade. Certain parts of the wall overlooked hotels and restaurants below; other sections protected pedestrians from sheer drops of a hundred feet or more. I needed a location away from the sunset throng so I could hide among the tourists without getting stuck in a crowd.

I chose a section of the promenade bordered by a cluster of shops on one side and a café and restaurant on the other. I tossed my personal phone into a trashcan next to the café and then slid back among the tourists who perused the nearby shops.

For an hour, I pretended to consider souvenirs and casual clothing, always within view of the café. Every few seconds, I glanced at the trashcan. A clerk became annoyed with me for loitering in her shop without buying anything. I grabbed two pairs of earrings the girls might like and asked her to ring them up. I stood at the register ready to hand over my card, and the giant Spiro from Theo Bakas's pleasure yacht strolled past the trashcan.

"I'm sorry," I said. "I'll have to return for the earrings. My friend just walked by."

"I can't hold them for you," she said, annoyed.

"Don't worry. I'll be back."

Adrenaline rushed through me. With a racing pulse, I hurried into the next shop, hid behind a postcard rack, and eyed Spiro.

He went into the café to search for me but soon exited to check the restaurant next door. A few seconds later, he came out and paused two feet from the trashcan to scan the promenade. He brought his hand to the side of his head to steady an earpiece so he could hear more clearly. At one point, he held his hands out to the side as if to say, "What do you want me to do? No one's here." Spiro waited a few seconds longer and then marched across the promenade toward a side street that led toward the parking areas.

So far so good.

I called Selene using the prepaid phone.

"He's coming," I said. "Get ready to meet me next to the bakery."

We had arranged earlier that she would wait in her car a few blocks away until I gave her directions. My initial plan was to borrow her car, but she insisted on staying with me. She knew the island better and had improved on my plan by asking a few of her friends to assist in the tailing of whoever tracked down my phone.

I kept a half a block between Spiro and me. He never even turned around to see if he was being followed. There were several lots for parking at the edge of the main road, and as we drew nearer, I closed my distance so I could identify his car. Away from the promenade, the crowd thinned out to just a few people. Selene stayed on the phone the whole way.

"He's turning left," I said. "He's probably in that lot across from the rental car office."

"I'm pulling closer now," she said.

I made the left turn, and a figure stepped toward me from a doorway. My eyes darted that way, and Markos swiped at me with a knife. My heart jumped, and I lunged backward, my chest and arms drawing away, desperate to be free of the arc of his swing. The razor sharp blade cut through the front of my shirt and skimmed the edge of my chest.

I yelped and struggled back a step. A slice of searing pain screamed for attention, but I stayed on my feet.

Markos had committed fully to his first swing and took a few moments to regain his balance. He maneuvered into position for another go, and I stepped farther away, my eyes locked on his knife.

In my years of boxing and martial arts, I had run into all kinds of fighting enthusiasts at the gym who liked to trade techniques. I once met a retired Special Forces guy who told me the only opponent he truly feared was a guy with a knife.

"You may think you can beat him with your moves," he had said, "but he'll rush you, put his arm around your back, and knife your gut four times before you cock your fist." He had preached the gun-or-run tactic of dealing with a knife wielder. "If you have a gun," he coached, "shoot him. If you don't, then run."

Markos took a small step toward me, and I crept backward. We were eight feet apart. His right hand held the knife low to his side, his left arm bent and in front of his face. He knew what he was doing, and when he took another step toward me, I turned and ran.

I sprinted toward the promenade, away from the direction Spiro had gone. After fifty paces, I hazarded a glance back. He was twenty strides behind me but losing ground; I slowed my pace because I needed Markos. I needed him alive and talking. If I could bait him to stay with me and wear him down with the chase, he wouldn't be as fast with the knife.

I dodged tourists, and they jumped back with surprised faces. At the promenade, I turned right in the direction of the sunset and looked back again. He maintained his speed, still quite determined. The walkway grew more crowded. I glanced again to make sure he could see me and then ducked into a fashion boutique with several entrances onto the promenade. Markos entered the store with a flourish, saw me, and shoved an elderly woman out of the way. I hurried across the width of the store and out onto the promenade again. Looking back, I realized late that he had left the store by another doorway. I turned. He was almost to me. I began running, but he had a faster start and would reach me in a few more steps. I passed the façade of the store and angled left across the promenade. The wall was only three feet tall there.

At the wall, I turned around, and he stopped a few feet from me. I had no room. If he lunged now, he would lock me up and shred my torso. I put both hands on the flat edge of the wall, leaped to the top, and faced him. His eyes grew wide in disbelief. One step back, and I would drop forty feet to a rooftop below. A woman screamed from the other side of the promenade. Markos slashed at me, and I jumped, my legs instinctively retracting above his swing. I landed back on the wall and did a shuffle. My weight leaned out a hair, and I swung my arms like a crazy cartoon character to regain my balance. He swiped again, higher this time. I hurled my legs to the side, and his knife creased my calf. I came down sideways on the wall, kicked him in the chest with my good foot, and started running in the direction from which we had come.

I limped slightly now, mostly for show, because adrenaline shielded me from the pain. I looked back again. The run had taken a lot out of Markos, and he slowed to a jog. I baited him by slowing further to let him close the distance. Up ahead was a small square with room to move. I would find a way to end it there. He was fifteen feet back when I turned left into the square. It was mostly deserted, as the tourists had gravitated toward the viewing spots.

His footsteps closed on me. Reaching the end of the square, I ran a half circle and headed out toward the promenade again without a clue of how to capture Markos without getting killed. I sped up and chanced a glimpse over my shoulder. He was three steps back . . . no time to stop and face him.

The wall was straight ahead, the end of the race. Thirty feet.

I counted my steps, one, two, three, four; then I lurched left and pivoted toward him, my weight falling. He dragged his feet, perhaps not sure he could stop in time. I grabbed his left forearm and yanked him along. Then I thrust my right hand to his belt and pushed him upward. I had hoped to slam his head into the wall, but I misgauged the angle. Markos's eyes bulged. His forward momentum, combined with the force of me pulling his arm, carried him into the wall. His thighs hit the top edge, and he tried to grab it with his right hand, but the knife got in the way of his grip. His center of gravity was above the wall, and his shoulders and head began to go over. I let go of his arm and belt, and that was it.

He was too out of breath to scream. He managed to whimper, "Hey," and nothing more.

I sat on the promenade with my back to the wall, my chest heaving, trying to take in what had happened. Then I stood to peer over the edge.

Markos was a crumpled mess on the rocks a hundred feet below. He lay on his back with his legs bent grotesquely behind him. One of his arms was on his stomach, and the other pointed to the side. In the fading light, I couldn't see his face. A wave of relief washed over me. His knife was gone. He was gone.

But so was my chance of finding Annie.

I turned and limped away with my hand across my middle to hide the blood from his first cut. A man and woman holding hands strolled toward the wall. They did not realize that Markos had fallen to his death.

"What happened?" the woman asked.

I ignored them and kept walking with my head lowered.

"Hey!" demanded the man. "What happened?"

They ventured closer to the wall. I hurried across the square and turned into an alleyway leading toward the main road. Then I called Selene to fetch me.

Chapter 26

SIX MEN ARRIVED at the back door of Selene's kitchen all at the same time. She let them in, and they stood lined along the countertop. I sat at the small dining table with my shirt off, a fresh bandage on my stomach. Selene had used scissors to cut my pants leg away, and after letting the men in the door, she propped my leg on a seat and cleaned the second wound. I was lucky; neither cut was deep.

The men watched Selene work and talked with her in Greek.

They all wore work clothes: heavy trousers, long-sleeved shirts, and caps. Scruffy beards covered their faces. They made soft noises as they settled in, shoes moving against the floor, backs leaning on the counter. Prolonged exposure to the sun had turned their faces and hands dark and leathery, rendering their ages indeterminate. They might have been anywhere from their late thirties to early sixties.

Selene introduced them, and they all stepped forward to shake my hand. I remembered the names Vasili and Kostas, but the others jumbled together in my head. They talked with Selene and gestured at me a few times. I got the impression they were trying to figure out how to help me.

Julian sat on the other side of the table and watched everything. He stayed silent, playing the respectful child, happy to be included as a listener.

Selene wiped the cut with a wet cloth.

"Ouch," I said. "That stings!"

One of the men chuckled.

"I have to clean it well," she said. "Infection is your only danger now."

"I get the feeling you might be enjoying it."

Julian laughed, and Selene shut him up with a glare.

"These men are all fishermen," she said. "Kostas is my uncle."

Kostas nodded.

"We have been debating where Theo Bakas might have taken your friend Annie. Bakas has many rental properties in Fira and other places on the island, too many for us to check. We don't even know them all."

Kostas said something, and the other men all began talking at once. Some nodded. Others shook their heads. One man touched his cap and pointed at the boots and pants of the man standing next to him.

Finally, Julian spoke to the room in Greek. He talked for the better part of a minute. It seemed to me that he wanted to help. Julian's great-uncle frowned, but the man next to him nodded.

Selene lifted her head, and her eyes searched mine.

"What?" I said.

"At first, Kostas suggested that they recruit more people they trust. Then they would fan throughout the island to search for Theo Bakas or his men, with most of them focusing on Fira. But then Vasili pointed out that they would be conspicuous in Fira, for as fishermen, they rarely come to the town."

"Yeah. I get that. If Bakas thinks he's being hunted, he might panic."

"But Julian wants to help. He says that he and his friends can move through Fira undetected. They go to town often, and they know all the backstreets and pathways."

"No," I said. "Bad idea." Pulling Selene's friends into the fight was one thing. They were grown men who knew about life and risks and downsides and scars. But kids? They believed they were immortal.

Julian spoke to his mother in Greek, his voice rushed and full of passion. They argued. She remained calm and reached to touch his arm. He spoke even faster. Two of the men standing at the counter nodded. Selene frowned and turned to face me again.

"As you can tell, Julian feels strongly about this. He says there is no danger."

"That's right," agreed Julian.

Selene signaled with her hand that he should stop talking. "He suggests that we buy more temporary phones. He will share them with his friends, and they will spread across Fira to form a sort of . . . community."

"A network," I said.

"Yes, a network. The boys will blend into the crowds and be quiet and unnoticed. If they see something, they will call you."

"I still don't like it," I said.

"Please, Joe," said Julian, his eyes earnest. "She's my friend too."

Kostas said something, and most of the standing men nodded.

"My uncle agrees with Julian," said Selene. "He thinks you should give Julian a chance." She gazed lovingly at her son. "And so do I."

Julian desperately wanted me to say yes, and his plan made sense. Adults went through their days focused on their own selfish little lives, while kids stood in the shadows and observed everything.

"Okay," I said to Julian, "but you must tell the other boys to call me if they see Bakas. They must not get involved. They are to walk away and call me. Understand?"

Julian nodded.

* * *

THE MEN LEFT to recruit other men. They planned to canvass the rest of the island. They would search for Bakas family vehicles or anything out of the ordinary. I gave Selene a bunch of cash to buy a dozen phones in Oia. Meanwhile, Julian used the landline to call his friends. He would form a group of ten to twelve boys to blanket Fira.

When Selene returned, she and I activated the phones and made sure Julian knew how they worked. Then Selene and two of the men shuttled the boys to Fira. As the hunted one, I changed into clean clothes and stayed put. I tried to contact Giorgos and the captain without luck. Finally, at eight o'clock, the captain called.

"I'm on the fast ferry," he said. "I'll be there in three hours."

I told him that Bakas had kidnapped Annie and that Markos had fallen to his death from the promenade in Oia.

"He fell?"

"Uh huh."

"You're saying it was an accident."

"I might have helped him a little."

Veggos spewed Greek curse words and then said, "Stay in hiding. I have two federal officers with me. With that show of force, the rest of the police will do their jobs, and we'll close this down."

"Three hours is a long time," I said. "I'm worried about Annie."

Background noise from the ferry came over the phone. I thought perhaps Veggos had gotten distracted, but I didn't hear him talking to anyone else.

"Hello?" I said.

"I'm here."

The ambient noise on his end increased. The ferry's engines had kicked on, but Veggos remained silent.

"What is it?" I said.

"One of my contacts in the federal office heard something late in the day. They have an informant inside the Bakas organization, but he's not that reliable. Word came that something bad had happened in Santorini but that everything would be cleaned up tonight, including the Americans."

Damn. Clean up the Americans. Annie and me. Perhaps my tough-guy routine had backfired, pressured Theo Bakas into acting rashly.

"Stay where you are," he reiterated. "Wait for me."

"Okay. I'll wait for now. But if one of my new friends finds Bakas, I'm going to check the situation out for myself."

An hour later, Julian called me.

"We found them," he said. "They're in an apartment in Fira two blocks from the town center."

"Stay back now."

"We are safe. My friend Zander and I are watching from behind a van on the street. Remember the big man we saw on the boat at the old port?"

"Yes."

"He comes onto the patio to smoke, goes back inside, and then ten minutes later, he comes out again."

"Where are you exactly?"

He gave me directions, and I told him we'd be there in twenty minutes.

Selene drove. She knew the way and had no sense of fear around the corners.

What the hell was I to do? I called the captain, but he must have been out of cell coverage. What did it mean when an unreliable informant said Theo Bakas planned to "clean up the Americans?" Would Bakas dare to hurt Annie before he knew my whereabouts? I rolled my shoulders and fidgeted in my seat. I couldn't plan the next move until I got a closer look.

Chapter 27

WE MET JULIAN and his friend Zander well after dark. They had changed position to get a better view of the apartment. They were now stationed at the railing of an open-air staircase that overlooked Bakas's place from a half block away. Zander, a stocky boy with the beginnings of a mustache, had first spotted the giant Spiro in the lights of the apartment's patio. I shook his hand and thanked him for helping.

The apartment had a door that opened onto the patio, but Spiro had not been out to smoke for twenty minutes. Were they still in there? From our position, I could make out indistinct shapes through the four apartment windows that bordered the patio. I trained my binoculars on the first window and saw an empty chair beside a dining table. The next window made my heart jump because Giorgos sat at the same table. I couldn't see enough of the room to know who else was there.

Was Giorgos partnering with Theo Bakas all along? Had he lied to me? It appeared so, but why hadn't he sent Bakas's men to get me at the condo in Oia? And more importantly, was Annie in that room? I had to get closer.

I gave Selene the captain's number and left her with the boys. They would keep an eye on my progress, and if anything unexpected happened, they would call for help.

I detoured a block out of the way to approach the condo from a different direction and then climbed the back stairs of the patio where Spiro had smoked. Large potted plants gave me places to hide twenty feet from the windows. Through sheer white curtains, I made out the figure of Giorgos sitting at the table, but the rest of the room was a blur. I approached the window next to Giorgos.

Giorgios appeared to be reading something with his head tilted toward the table. I stepped closer. In the few minutes I had watched him from the patio, he hadn't pulled on his ear or scratched his neck or turned his head. I moved to within two feet of the window. The back of his head appeared odd, and a dark trail ran down his neck like a still, shiny rattail.

A chill ran up my spine to the back of my neck. I finally saw the gunshot wound; Giorgos was dead. I held my breath, and my head jerked left and right to check the empty patio.

Inside the room, someone talked in a low voice. A man stood on the other side of the table, but I could not see him clearly through the curtains. The room was rectangular, with more windows on a wall around the corner from me. Perhaps those windows would afford me a better view.

The potted plants bordered the edges of the patio all the way around. I stepped lightly around the corner and then leaned to peer through another window. Theo Bakas paced back and forth on the opposite side of the room. He waved his arms and lectured to Spiro, who was sitting at the end of the table. Neither of them paid any attention to the dead Giorgos.

Then something cold and hard pressed into my neck.

"Don't move, Mr. Robbins, or I will shoot you in the back of the head."

My heart's pump cranked to the max. I froze in place and then slowly put my hands to the side.

"Okay," I said.

"Good. Let's walk this way."

It was the son, Dorian Bakas. He led me through a door and along a short hallway. Plodding in a daze with my heart still racing, I tried to steady my breath to clear my mind.

Theo Bakas started when we entered the room. His eyes grew wide at the sight of me, and then he smiled, visibly relieved.

"What's this? The elusive Mr. Robbins. The man bearing threats of my imminent demise. Excellent work, Dorian. Was anyone with him?"

"No. He came alone."

"Fantastikós!"

What a colossal screwup. Selene and the boys would have watched me looking in the first window on the patio, but after I moved around the corner, they could no longer see me. For all they knew, I remained safely hidden. What would they do?

Theo gestured to a seat. "Please, join us. Have a cold beer. Spiro, fetch one. We were just debating next moves, but Dorian has made the way forward much clearer."

I sat, my mind moving slowly. Spiro placed an open bottle of Mythos in front of me, and I surreally took a sip. *This could be my last beer.* I hardly tasted it.

Theo sat two seats away from me and nodded happily. "Oh, where are our manners? Spiro, the snacks. Yes, the plate there." Spiro took the plate and pushed it toward me: dolmades, puff pastries, pita chips, and hummus.

"There you go," said Theo. "Eat. Not hungry? Well, it doesn't matter much anyway. Not like you're a growing boy. Ha!"

"Where is Annie?"

"She is safe." His eyebrows furrowed, and he frowned. "I took your suggestions seriously." Then he shrugged. "Spiro had other ideas, and he works hard and deserves a special reward now and then, but I said, 'No, we must wait to see what happens. You can't be too careful.'" Theo sat straight and took a deep breath. "Now Markos, he is a different story. I would never have allowed Markos to touch her. In fact, I thank you for disposing of Markos. He had grown unreliable. It was the drugs." Theo shook his head as if distressed. "You think you have opioid problems in the US, but they're *everywhere* now, even in the islands. It's terrible!"

While he talked, my mind shifted to a higher gear. Where was Annie? Was she truly safe? What should I do?

Dorian stood in the corner with a weak smile on his face. He stared at empty air in front of him, then glanced at his father every few seconds.

Spiro stood on the other side of Theo and wolfed down a mountain of appetizers from a plate.

Theo strode to his son and said, "Give me the gun." Then he gave Dorian rapid instructions in Greek. He said the word *skáfos* twice, which I knew meant boat.

Dorian said, "Okay," and immediately left the room, and Theo returned to his seat.

Were they hiding Annie on the luxury yacht?

I was down to two opponents, and only one of them, Theo, had a gun. Could I rush him? No. Theo would shoot me before I could reach him. At the least, he would hold me off until Spiro grabbed me. Spiro would snap my neck like a matchstick. He was NFL-lineman big. Three hundred pounds and more, with massive shoulders and arms. His triple-X shirt stretched tight across his chest muscles.

"You are checking out Spiro, I see." Theo tapped the side of his head with the barrel of his gun. "You're smart. Very smart. You assess the situation. You're in danger, and you believe I mean to kill you. That is my logical next step. So, what should you do? Make a move for the pistol. But there is Spiro. He is huge and might kill you himself. He will certainly kill you if I ask him to."

"Annie knows nothing about the wastewater project," I said. "Now that you have me, you can let her go."

Theo slammed the table. Spiro paused in his eating and arched his eyebrows.

"That damn wastewater project!" said Theo. He pointed the barrel at the dead Giorgos. "My friend for fifty years is dead because of that stupid project and my stupid son. Giorgos and I played in school like brothers. Football. We both loved football."

Theo sat six feet from me, and he laid the gun on the table. "Oh, my son, my son, my stupid, stupid son." He tilted his head toward me. "You didn't help either, with your snooping. Giorgos insisted I repay the money. 'Of course,' I said. 'But I need some time.' Dorian lost the money in Monaco. Stupid, I know, very stupid. What can I do? I don't have four million euros lying around. 'Then Dorian has to go to jail,' said Giorgos. He kept saying that. Yesterday and then today. I got tired of it. He refused to listen, so I had Spiro shoot him. My friend."

His eyes were downcast and his face muscles slack. He rubbed his hands together and shook his head. "Damn Americans. You guys ruin everything with your spreadsheets and your clouds and your vegan diets. Yuck. What is happening to the world?"

"I could help you," I said, desperate, willing to try anything. "Let me run the management company. I've got the experience. I can move the numbers around enough to confuse any auditor, which would give you time to get the money. Think about it. This is a win-win."

He burst out laughing, his shoulders shaking. "A win-win?" He kept laughing, and I slumped. "You're something else, Joe. Something else." He wiped at his eyes.

Okay. My options were limited. Lunge for the gun. I had a slim chance of getting there before Spiro reacted, but Spiro was fast. He was eating but attentive. With his massive hand, he would grab my arm, twist it, and dislocate my shoulder.

"I used to like Americans," said Theo. "You're very clever. When I was Dorian's age, I chased every American girl I saw, and I caught a few right here in Santorini. Then came the Athens Olympics in 2004. They were going to restore Greece to the greatness of the ages. We bet our future, borrowed nine billion we didn't have to build the infrastructure. You know how many gold medals we won? Six. Gamó! The Americans won twice that many in swimming alone. Our men's football team didn't make it to the quarterfinals."

"There must be a deal we can work out," I said, still desperate.

Theo's eyes went wild, still stuck in 2004. "Yes, an Olympic competition. I'll give you a fair chance to go free." His eyes darted to Spiro, who put his now empty plate on a side table. "You box Spiro. Right here. Right now."

Theo translated his proposal for Spiro, who immediately began to remove his clothes. He stripped off his shirt to reveal a massive torso devoid of hair. Then he sat on a chair to remove his shoes.

"I'd hardly call that fair," I said.

Theo screamed, "Was the US against Greece fair? With your resources? Your unlimited funds? Your Michael Phelps? To heck with fair." He pointed his pistol at me. The barrel wiggled with his trembling. "You want the fight?"

"Yes."

A sitting room abutted the dining area, and Spiro began to move furniture to the side. The open area in the middle was slightly larger than a boxing ring. I stood and walked to the open space.

Theo stayed by the table and began talking in Greek as if he were a sports announcer sharing pre-match color commentary. Spiro moved the last upholstered chair off to the side.

"Joe," said Theo, and I looked at him. "We're going to dispense with the handshake if you don't mind."

From behind me came a light step and an intake of breath. I ducked and jumped right, and Spiro swung his closed fist through open air. Theo switched back to Greek, his voice rising to announce a failed surprise attack.

I came up on my toes. Spiro turned to face me and swiped an open palm at my temple. I rocked back out of the way and then jabbed him twice. He shook the punches off like a dog shakes off water.

He stepped toward me, and I circled to his right.

Excitement filled Theo's voice, and he chattered nonstop.

Spiro swiped at me again, missed, and I landed a straight right to the side of his face. His head snapped back, and he blinked hard. With a few more of those, I would start to make progress. But Spiro was smarter than I thought.

He wound up for a haymaker right but stalled it halfway then punched straight out with his left. His fist caught my mouth and sent me sprawling to the floor. I slid and crashed into a buffet and hutch with glass-fronted doors. With Spiro stomping toward me, I grabbed a footstool and hurled it at his head. He paused to brush the stool to the side, and I scrambled to my feet.

Spiro abandoned all pretext of boxing and rushed me. I stepped to the side, but he reached his long arm to corral me. He hurled me, and I crashed into the hutch, shattering the front panes.

I bounced off and caught him by surprise, punched him three times hard in the face. Spiro stepped back, stunned. Theo changed his tone, doubt creeping in about the champ's expected victory. My lip was bleeding; otherwise, I felt okay. I bounced on my toes, ready for him. He moved toward me gingerly, his head tilted back, wary of my fists.

"Bring it," I said.

His leg moved quickly, faster than I could see; he roundhouse-kicked me behind my knees and knocked me to the ground. I rolled away from him, cocked my leg, and when he came closer, I jabbed my foot against his ankle. His three hundred pounds crashed against the floor. The building shuddered, and the windows rattled.

Theo howled his dismay.

I scrambled to Spiro and straddled his chest with my knees pinning his shoulders. I put my hands on his neck, rocked up, and let all my weight press through my arms and against his throat.

Theo hovered close by, his voice rising, his words warning of potential calamity.

Spiro grabbed my forearms with his massive hands, but I had too much leverage on him. As I squeezed, his face turned red.

I had him. I knew it. I was going to strangle him right there.

Theo continued to announce the fight in a steady drone, but I ignored him. Spiro's face turned darker. I breathed hard through my nose. My arms shook.

Spiro had hauled Constantine to the peak of Skaros Rock and thrown him over the side. If given a chance, he would sexually assault Annie. Theo wouldn't let me go free. When the fight was over, he would kill me, but I could keep Spiro from hurting Annie.

Theo spewed angry commentary, but his voice faded as I squeezed.

Then Spiro relaxed his grip on my arms. He raised his eyebrows as if a new thought had entered his brain.

Theo picked up on it. Wait, fans, hold on a second.

Spiro stretched his arms out far to the side and then slammed his fists against my temples. My ears rang and my head bobbled, but I held onto his throat. Theo shouted with glee. Spiro stretched his arms out again, arched his chest to give himself more leverage, and I knew what was coming. Spiro delivered a second crushing blow to my temples, and I lost my grip on his throat. Theo went wild, loudly predicting the champ's victory. Spiro slammed me from the right, and I rolled across the floor.

My mind reeled from the pain. I stumbled to my feet, my eyes unfocused. Spiro coughed and struggled to catch his breath, then turned on his side and stood. My right ear bled from a tear. The room swirled. My left knee wobbled, and I almost fell. I made fists and raised them but wasn't sure I could swing my arm. Theo's voice rose in anticipation.

Spiro reached his full height. Yes, he was a giant. My shoulders swayed.

His punch crashed into the side of my face. I fell, and Theo shouted, "Goal! Goal! Goal!"

Chapter 28

I CAME TO WITH A HEADACHe that kept me on the lingering edge of consciousness for several minutes. My body swayed with a rocking motion, and I slowly grew aware of my physical predicament. My arms, shoulders, and head were upside down, my torso and waist were stretched over the top of something, and my legs hung off the other side. Whoever had bound me so—Spiro probably—had tied my hands together and loosely wrapped me in a sheet.

A pungent odor filled the surrounding air. The gentle rocking continued, and the cut on my stomach burned as it rubbed against the saddle. The donkey walked slowly on a concrete path in the eerie light cast by the moon. My body was held in place by a rope that ran from my hands under the donkey to my feet on the other side. We wound our way down the switchbacks to the bottom of the cliffs of Fira.

A second donkey tromped in front of mine, and two men murmured in Greek while the animals clip-clopped on the walkway. They must not have expected me to regain consciousness soon, for they had not gagged me, but that revelation did me little good. Yelling for help would only earn me a quick bash on the head.

I tried to relax and breathed deeply of air thickened by the smell of manure. We made a final turn, leveled out onto the wide concrete deck, and trudged a couple hundred feet before stopping. Then another man's voice greeted the donkey tenders. Water gently lapped against the side of a vessel. An inboard boat engine idled smoothly. There was a friendly dispute between the three men, and then they laughed quietly as if they did not wish to disturb anyone who might be still lingering on the dockside.

The man on the boat was Spiro, and he gave the others instructions as he untied a burden from the lead donkey. I got the impression he was teaching the other two how to unload this sort of cargo. Spiro grunted when he shifted Giorgos's corpse from the animal's back to his own, and then he called to one of the men for assistance.

The two men struggled as they stepped from the dock onto the boat, and then Giorgos thumped on the deck like a sack of dirt. They'd be back for me next. I tried to relax every fiber in my body so I would appear as dead as Giorgos.

Spiro undid the rope that ran between my hands and feet, lifted me halfway off the donkey, and wedged his right shoulder into the gap between my chest and the saddle. He called out, and one of the men came to support my upper legs as they were pulled over the top of the donkey. They carried me unsteadily across the dockside and down three steps into the boat. With a heave, Spiro let me drop to the deck. My shoulders landed on Giorgos, and I rolled off to lie beside him. Spiro gave me a half-hearted kick in the side to make sure I was still out.

The men exchanged a few words, and the other two got off the boat. Sure footsteps walked to and fro on the deck, and then I heard the sound of a rope hitting the dockside. Soon after, the engine revved, and the boat pulled away from the dock.

Of course, they had to dispose of the bodies: Giorgos, Annie, and me. With the right amount of anchor weight, a corpse would sink and be eaten by other creatures long before humans discovered it. I shivered at the thought of such a cold and dark end.

Now that he had captured me, Theo would allow Spiro to have his way with Annie. She might be on the yacht a dozen feet from where I lay. Who else was on board?

I opened my eyes as slits. They had tossed Giorgos and me side by side onto the main deck of the boat. Giorgos lay in front of me, and I lifted my head only enough to see over his shoulder. Spiro stood at the captain's wheel steering the craft farther into the caldera. We were on the luxury yacht I had seen at the dockside a few days earlier. The shiny, varnished gunwales reflected moonlight.

Footsteps climbed from the below deck cabin, and I lowered my head. Theo and Spiro exchanged words in Greek. Soft footsteps approached me, and I imagined Theo staring at Giorgos and me. Would he kill me now? Perhaps stab me with the fish gaff? Why bother? Why create a mess on his deck when he could easily have Spiro toss me into the sea alive? What about Annie? Would he give her a merciful, quick death after Spiro had assaulted her? Why bother with that either?

Theo turned and walked away. A moment later, he issued a few short instructions to Spiro and went back below deck. Spiro throttled the engine higher. The seas were calm in the caldera, and the boat cruised smoothly forward.

My arms were bound together at the wrists with nylon rope a quarter inch thick. I twisted my hands in opposite directions with no success. Spiro knew his knots.

I moved my arms across my waist and located a small metal instrument of hope inside my jeans. No one carried pocketknives anymore. On a street in the US, the person next to you was more likely carrying a handgun than a knife. Why even bother to check? Spiro must have felt the same way.

It took several minutes to work the Leatherman to the top of my pocket, then I promptly dropped it onto the deck.

I froze.

Whew. Spiro could hear little over the rumble of the engines. My hands shook as I anxiously worked to open the outer blade. Getting the knife into position to saw at the rope was awkward, but when I finally figured out how to do it, the sharp edge sliced through the nylon in seconds. I drew a deep, quiet breath, lifted my head to see Spiro staring ahead through the windshield, and then crunched up to cut the ropes around my feet.

Then I lowered my shoulders to think. I had a few seconds of surprise to work with. If I made a loud noise or moved too quickly, Spiro would sense something had changed and turn around. I had to overpower him in an instant, or the ensuing fight would play out as it had in the sitting room. To do that, I needed a more serious weapon than a pocketknife.

My eyes swiveled a few feet above my head to the fish gaff hanging underneath the gunwale. The gaff was six feet long with a five-inch gap between the shank and the sharp end of the hook. I had once seen a first mate on a fishing charter gaff a huge yellowfin tuna in one swift move. But it was an awkward instrument. Could I slug Spiro over the head with it? No. The handle was too narrow. If I missed and hit his shoulder, he would shrug off the blow and smash my face.

I closed my eyes to imagine what Spiro would do to Annie before weighing her down with an anchor and lowering her over the side.

I stretched my feet and legs, swiveled my ankles a few times, and then softly rose and crept to the gaff. Spiro hummed a song under the noise of the engine, and I lifted the gaff from its holder. It felt solid and sure in my hands. The polished steel sparkled. I soft stepped toward him with adrenaline cranking through my body and my heart pounding at my chest.

Closer. Closer. One quick movement.

I looped the hook over his shoulder to the front of his neck and yanked back with all my strength. The point of the gaff protruded from the back of Spiro's upper spine. Blood from his throat splashed against the windshield. He took two hesitant steps backward, and his knees gave out.

I dropped the gaff and reached for his arm, struggling to slow his descent and lighten the sound of his fall. He crumpled against the gunwale, and I stared at him, unable to breathe. His front was a bloody mess. He flapped his arms against the deck for a few loud seconds and then was still.

I blinked and blinked, my mind frozen by the violence. My shoulders swayed a moment, but then I snapped alert.

Had Theo noticed the noise downstairs?

The bow drifted slightly right, and I grabbed the wheel to straighten it.

We were passing out of the north end of the caldera. Lights shone from the clifftop at Oia. I searched the instruments of the dash—bloody switches. There might have been an autopilot, but I couldn't sort it out. I'd have to hope we didn't drift off course enough to attract attention.

I crept to the opening that led below. At the foot of the steps was a shadowed hallway. Light and a low voice came from a forward room. It sounded like a television show.

At least one other person had a gun on the boat. I needed another weapon, and removing the gaff from Spiro was not an option.

I tiptoed to the bench at the stern, lifted a hatch, and removed the contents: two life jackets and a short length of rope. The life jackets gave me an idea. If I could sneak Annie onto the deck, we could strap on the jackets and swim to shore. Oia was a half-mile away but growing more distant with each moment. I placed the life jackets on the seat and carried the rope with me. At the door, I decided the cord would only get in my way in a fight, so I left it on the deck.

The full moon was high overhead. For a moment, I thought I heard the sound of another engine, but when I searched the waters behind and beside us, I saw nothing, and then the sound faded.

I gingerly climbed down the steps to the lower floor. The narrow hallway led to a sitting room where a television played, and two men talked in low voices: Theo and Dorian. To my right was a closed door.

Staying in the shadows, I crept up the hallway until I could peek into the sitting room. A soccer match played on a widescreen television mounted on the forward wall. Behind the television were shelves lined with books. Theo sat on a sofa facing away from me and nibbled on snacks while he watched. A sullen and tired Dorian sat in an armchair on the right.

I moved back to the door next to the steps. The handle turned, and inside I found a small dark room. Dim moonlight slipped in through a porthole, and a figure lay prone on a bunk.

The woman was awake and tried to speak, but her voice was muffled. I knelt beside her, and she shrank back. Her arms and legs were tied to the farthest ends of the bunk. Her face was indistinguishable in the shadows, but I recognized her curly hair.

"Annie." I reached to touch her arm, and she jerked. "It's Joe."

She breathed a huge sigh of relief.

"There's no time," I said. "And I can't risk the light."

She was fully dressed in jeans and a long-sleeved shirt. My fingers traced the contours of her face and felt the tape they'd used to seal her mouth shut.

"Shh."

I managed to untie one hand, but then a loud voice sounded from the sitting room. I stood and stepped to the door.

Theo gave instructions to Dorian. When Dorian's voice disagreed, Theo shouted, and I heard the name Spiro.

My heart raced. Annie was within reach, but I guessed that Theo had told his son to go topside.

"Annie," I whispered. "I have to go. I'll be back in a minute."

Without listening for her response, I closed the door and hustled up the steps.

What to do now? Spiro lay in a large puddle of blood beneath the wheel. Dorian might or might not bring a gun, but he was bound to yell as soon as he noticed Spiro's corpse. I glanced at the short length of rope, and Dorian's shoe touched the first step. I reached for the cord, stood with my back against the forward wall next to the doorway, and wrapped the ends of the line around my hands.

The noise of a second boat engine—closer now—came aboard with the breeze. I glanced back but still didn't see anything in the dark.

Dorian reached the top, gaped at Spiro and all the blood, and opened his mouth to yell.

I looped the rope over his head and turned around so that the two ends twisted and lay over my shoulder. Then I lifted Dorian off the ground by his neck.

He went crazy, kicking and flailing. At first, his struggling almost brought me down, but then I leaned forward at the waist for more leverage. I crept to the middle of the deck, took deep breaths, and waited. Dorian reached for his neck. Realizing he couldn't move the rope, he scratched at me with his fingers, but he was losing strength by then. In another minute, he stopped struggling, and I lowered him to lie beside Giorgos.

In all the excitement, I had lost track of my immediate surroundings, but I now noticed that the steering wheel had turned sharply to port. Then Theo popped his head out from the doorway.

His dead son lay at my feet, and when he saw me standing and Dorian prone, he shouted and pulled at his waistband for his gun.

I instinctively moved away and toward the stern. Under the low light of the wheelhouse, the skin on his face drew tight. With teeth bared, he raised his pistol to shoot me.

I grabbed one of the life jackets from the seat and threw it at him. The jacket hit him on the chest at the same time he fired, and the shot went wide. I reached for the second life jacket, and the moment felt surreal, like Theo and I were competing in an absurd arcade game. I almost laughed. The second jacket hit him on the gun hand, and again his shot missed.

But I was fresh out of life jackets. Theo raised his handgun again, and I dove right. The pistol fired, something tugged at my shirt, and my head crashed into the side of the boat. I lay on the deck, unmoving, dizzy, my vision blurring. The sound of the other boat was closer, but not close enough. The cavalry would not arrive in time. Theo stepped toward me, gun raised, and something hit the back of his head. A large book fell to the deck.

Annie.

Theo whirled and fired two shots toward the empty doorway. He ran to the door but changed his mind and came back to me. When he aimed his pistol again, a dark spot the size of a quarter appeared on his white shirt. He stumbled backward, and two more spots appeared near the first.

I detected the soft footfall of an experienced seaman coming aboard. Then I passed out.

Chapter 29

I CAME TO BRIEFLY when Captain Veggos and another man helped me move from the yacht to a boat that had been tied alongside. They laid me on a bench next to the rail. The craft smelled of dried fish and saltwater. A ringing sound in my ear nearly drowned out the lapping of water at the side of the boat. Annie knelt beside me with her brow wrinkled and a pained look in her eyes.

"Are you okay?" she said.

"Never better."

Tension melted from my torso, and my arm fell from the bench. Annie sat stiff and silent beside me. I wanted to comfort her, but the weight of a thousand years held me down. The engine revved, we motored away from the yacht, and I fell into a dark and soundless sleep.

I regained consciousness again when Annie and the man who piloted the boat helped me climb onto a dock. We stumbled a few hundred feet to a waiting car. We were in Ammoudi Bay and passed by several restaurants that had closed for the night. Soft waves splashed the shore. They tucked me into the passenger seat of a small truck. The engine whined as we climbed a steep hill, and I couldn't keep my eyes open any longer.

* * *

SOMETIME LATER, a bright overhead light switched on, and I blinked to full alertness. My brain throbbed with each heartbeat, and the piercing pain forced my eyes shut again for a moment. I was seated beside Selene next to her small dining table. We were alone. Annie and Julian talked loudly in the next room.

"There you are," she said.

"Here I am."

She stood close by and pulled my hair away to examine my upper forehead.

"You have a lump the size of a rock on your head," she said.

"Feels like a boulder."

She dabbed at the lump with a warm damp cloth. My shoulders wavered, and I put my arm around her hip for support. She laughed and moved closer.

"You like me now, don't you?" she said. "Now that you've knocked yourself senseless."

"I've always liked you."

"Quiet, you foolish American. Before you say something stupid."

After carefully taping an awkward bandage into place, Selene poured me a cup of black coffee, which seemed illogical given the time, but the coffee tasted better than any I could remember. I examined the two holes in the side of my shirt and marveled that the bullet had passed between my torso and arm without touching me.

I sensed the corners of my mouth turning up. Selene leaned against the counter with her arms crossed. She giggled and shook her head.

"Stop smiling," she said. "You look silly."

Her uncle and another man entered through the back door, and Selene poured them coffee. What the hell time was it? I checked my pockets for a phone but found only my Leatherman. Did these men never sleep? Her uncle said something and gestured at me. The other man laughed.

"My uncle says you look exhausted," Selene said. "They're going to take you and Annie back to the hotel."

Chapter 30

ANNIE AND I SLEPT in and spent the day lounging under an awning beside the pool. In the early afternoon, Julian brought us sandwiches and beer.

Annie was physically fine. Spiro had frightened her badly by coming into the cabin on the boat several times and staring at her without saying a word, breathing heavily. She had cringed on the bunk, afraid he would assault her, but he had always left after a few minutes.

The lump on my head was tender to the touch. My headache settled into a steady pain that I could mostly ignore as long as I wore sunglasses. When the sun had crossed four-fifths of the sky, we cleaned up and went to dinner at a nearby restaurant with a fantastic view.

After we ordered food, Annie called home to explain the situation with her ex-boyfriend Matt. Her parents said they would move two thousand dollars into her account to finance the rest of her trip—an early graduation present. She didn't bother them with the story of being kidnapped.

"They'd only worry," she said.

"For good reason," I said.

"It was a freak occurrence, and you know it."

In the morning, we walked to buy souvenir buttons, and then I took Annie to the airport. She knew three girls on a Eurail Pass trip. They were headed for Munich, and she would hurry to catch them.

"I have a few more museums and churches to tour," she said.

"Good for you."

* * *

I SPENT THE REST of the day helping Selene in the lobby. Giorgos's sister and her husband would come to Santorini in a few days to begin the process of settling Giorgos's affairs. Selene hoped they would keep her on at the hotel and perhaps make her the manager. I taught her how to use the systems I had come to know during my investigation.

It was close quarters behind the desk. Our chairs were nudged together, and as I walked her through screens on the monitor, she leaned against me to get a better look. She wore a mid-length loose skirt and sandals. Her toenails were painted red.

After a while, we took a break, and I stood to stretch. Keeping my feet stationary, I turned my shoulders away from Selene to work the muscles in my back. When I turned back toward her, she slipped into my arms, and we kissed.

The kiss lingered for a few seconds, then I buried my nose in her hair. It was heaven, just a hint of lavender. She pulled tight against my chest and then stepped back and glanced at the door.

"We have to work," she said.

"I know."

"Giorgos's sister is coming on Thursday."

I nodded at the screen. "Let's get to it."

We pulled our chairs together again, but my mind was distracted.

"Would you like to join me for dinner?" I said.

She cocked her head and raised her eyebrows. "It was only a kiss."

"I know. I know. You hate all Americans."

"*Almost* all Americans," she said to correct me. "Dinner would be fine. But don't get the wrong notion. I'm probably not going to sleep with you."

Probably? My standing had improved almost beyond comprehension.

"Excellent," I said. "Just dinner is great, because I hate to eat alone."

Chapter 31

CAPTAIN VEGGOS CAME to see me late that afternoon. I was sitting beside the pool with a cold beer. I had two more beers chilled in the ice bucket, and he accepted one when I offered.

In casual khakis and a white shirt with an open collar, he took a long pull. The air was hot, and we moved under one of the umbrellas for the shade.

"I must thank you, Joe," he said. "Your visit has been helpful to me."

"How's that?"

"I've made new friends on Santorini . . . the fishermen of Oia, Selene, and the boys. Those contacts will help me a great deal."

"So how did you find the boat?"

"After you left Julian and Zander on the staircase, the other boys gathered to observe Bakas's apartment from several vantage points. Two of them watched Spiro carry you to the donkey and begin the descent. They told Selene, and Selene called me, but without the fishermen . . ." He shook his head.

I asked him about the rest, but he wouldn't give me a straight answer.

"There is big news in Santorini this week," he said. He sat in a chair with his right ankle across his left knee and played with his shoe. "One of the local businessmen perished in a boat fire five miles out to sea. Apparently, his son and two friends were also on board. By the time another boat arrived to help, the vessel had sunk in a thousand feet of water."

"Santorini style," I said.

He shook his head. "The sea is cruel. She holds many secrets. Countless ships have carried their final stories to the bottom."

It made sense. This ending would have far less impact on the island economy. A mismanaged public project and a squabble among locals could be finessed in many ways.

"This kind of thing happens every year in the Mediterranean," said the captain. "A wealthy amateur gets drunk aboard his yacht, and something goes wrong. It's a tragedy."

The captain finished his beer and stood. He surveyed the view of Skaros Rock, Kea Nameni, and the caldera. Then he gave me a tight smile and said, "Enjoy the rest of your holiday. Perhaps you'll forgive me for saying I hope we don't meet again, at least not in an official capacity."

* * *

SELENE AND I went for dinner that night and two more times over the following week.

On a subsequent night, after I had dined alone, I sat in my room reading when a knock sounded at the door.

She stood in black leggings and a pink top with her arms crossed. Her arms came uncrossed, and she fidgeted with the hemline of her top.

"I've changed my mind," she said.

"About what?"

Her brows scrunched together, and she stared at me as if I were the dumbest guy in the room, which of course, I was.

"Oh," I said. "Please, come in."

I had imagined what it would be like, had fantasies of lovemaking the likes of which the Greek gods had never known. Reality never lives up to fantasy. We were only human, but neither of us seemed to mind.

We hung out as much as we could for the rest of my time in Santorini. On her days off, we went to the beach and sat under thatch umbrellas and read books with the sound of the surf in the background. After the beach, we would shower and have fresh seafood at a restaurant in Ammoudi Bay. Sometimes Julian tagged long. He was content that his mother had found brief happiness in the arms of an American.

Tension began to build in me as the day approached when Chandler and Callie would return from Colorado to Austin. I missed them badly. Video calls and texts would only take you so far.

On a Tuesday, Selene and I went to the beach at Vlychada. We rented chairs and then ran straight into the sea. I steadied her in the water as she floated, and then I kissed her softly.

Back at the chairs, I couldn't focus on my book. I had to leave for home on Friday.

"Selene?" I said.

"I know," she said. "I have a son and must stay here. You have two daughters and must leave to be with them. But not today."

I studied her perfect face, her nose and lips, her eyes—soft now that the fire was banked—and her delightfully fine dark hair.

"Let us enjoy today as if it could last forever."

Chapter 32

THE GIRLS WERE to stay with me for a long weekend, and I met them at the Grove. Rose joined us for dinner.

When she first saw me standing at the entrance, Callie ran to give me the biggest hug. "Too long, Daddy. Too long." I could have sworn she had grown during our six weeks apart. Chandler, too, although in her case it was less about height and more about filling out curves, becoming more woman and less girl.

My throat grew tight. "Yes. It was too long."

"Next year, we'll split our time between Mommy and you." Callie nodded solemnly as if she had a surefire cure. "Three weeks in Colorado and three weeks in Santorini."

"That could work," I said.

"Hmpf," said Chandler, her dark eyes playful. "You won't go to Santorini again. Next year it'll be Key West or Kathmandu or no place at all."

"It's good to see you, Chandler. I missed you too."

It was over ninety degrees, but we sat outside under the sprawling live oak. The dense shade cut the heat, and large fans stirred the air enough to make it pleasant.

We ordered salads and pizza to share, and Rose and I had wine. She seemed tense and drank her wine faster than usual. Her eyes drifted off to the side, and she lost track of the conversation a couple times.

I doubted the tension had anything to do with me. We had reconciled our conflicts long ago—we still loved each other but could never be together again because she had married someone else. Thinking about it made my chest ache. The girls recounted their summer adventures—mountain biking, hikes, and trout fishing. I hardly heard them. I wanted to stand, rush around the table behind Rose, and massage the tension from her shoulders.

After dinner, I asked the girls to run outside and play with their phones while Rose and I chatted. They were used to that request—responsible divorced parents often need a few minutes alone to discuss practical matters.

I switched seats to be next to Rose.

"What's going on?" I said.

"What do you mean?"

She lifted her wine glass, then realized the second one she'd ordered was already empty.

"Stuff like that," I said. "You're not here. I know that look. Your mind's swirling with worry."

She shook her head briefly, her eyes sharp now, trying to recover.

"It's nothing."

"Don't do that," I said. "Don't shut me out."

I reached for her hand. She grabbed mine and squeezed tightly.

Her eyes locked on me as she searched for the right words. She opened her mouth to speak, then closed it again. Her shoulders leaned toward me slightly, and her chin trembled.

"What?" I said.

"Dave might be cheating on me."

I sat straight with my eyes wide. No way. Not Dave Moreton. I'd rarely met a steadier hand in my life. I actually liked the guy— the man who married the woman I loved. He worked hard. He cared for the kids. He made a lot of money, and his body was unmarred by the scars of bullet wounds.

"Why do you say that?" I asked.

Rose slumped. "I don't know. I have no hard evidence, but he missed two weekends in Colorado. Said he had too much work happening here."

"Maybe that's true."

"That's not the worst part."

"Okay."

Her lower teeth bit into her upper lip so hard I thought she might draw blood. She twisted her hands together until the skin turned white.

"Go ahead," I said. "Tell me."

"It's just . . ." Her hands bunched into fists and shook. "He doesn't want to *do it* anymore."

Do what? I wondered, for an instant, and then I figured it out. Sex. Which stunned me. What straight man wouldn't want to have sex with Rose every minute he could? I wanted to make love to her every time I saw her. Maybe she was right. Maybe Dave was cheating.

"When did you last?" I said.

"I can't remember, it's been so long. Maybe the first week in Colorado. Maybe earlier than that. He missed a weekend visit, and I expected him to be randy the next time he came, but nothing happened. I've tried coming on a few times, but all I get is the 'I'm tired, rain check' line."

I felt my face scrunching and wiped my hand across my eyes to hide my incredulity. The conversation had gone way weird. How was I to respond? My ex-wife was sharing the details of her troubled sex life. Isn't that what girlfriends were for? A smartass remark came to me—I'd be happy to stand in, honey—but I instantly discarded it.

"How can I help?" I said.

Her head jiggled to indicate there was nothing I could do, but then her eyes widened with a new thought. She fidgeted with her earring.

"Maybe you could find out," she said. "Get some evidence one way or the other. That would help."

"You mean spy on Dave?"

She nodded so slightly I could hardly detect the movement. That's precisely what she meant.

"Rose, I'm not a detective."

"I can't hire a real detective. Dave's profile in the city is too visible. If word got out I suspected . . . that could hurt him badly. He might lose his partnership."

She had a good point. Success in commercial real estate has a lot to do with relationships. A tarnished brand could cost a brokerage firm a lot of money.

"Will you do it?" she said.

"Yes."

The word came out of my mouth before I had even considered her proposal. I regretted it immediately.

"I mean, maybe," I said. "It's a strange request. You've got to admit . . ."

"I know." She took my hand, and her fingers curled around mine. "I'm sorry, but I could never trust anyone else with this."

"Let me think on it a bit."

* * *

THE GIRLS RAN ahead to get to the Jeep, squabbling along the way over who got to ride shotgun. I opened the Lexus door for Rose and waited for her to start the engine. She rolled down the window and smiled.

Her lovely hands clenched the steering wheel but then relaxed. She gazed at me with soft brown eyes lightened with flecks of gold on the edges of the irises.

"You look good," she said. "Island life agrees with you."

I put my hands on the door. "You look good too."

Then she reached to touch me as a lover might. She felt my cheek and caressed my earlobe.

"Come here," she said.

I glanced at the Jeep and leaned in the window.

Her lips were hungry. She reached behind my neck to pull me closer, opening her mouth. Then she pulled away and wiped at her eyes with her hands. She shifted into reverse and took her foot off the brake. The silver sedan cruised out of the parking slot, and she switched into drive.

"See ya, Joey."

The End.

BONUS MATERIAL

The Island Thief came in shorter than the other Joe Robbins thrillers, so I have added a bonus story, *Fresh Faces and Crisp Uniforms,* which is an excerpt from a longer collection. *The Sheila Stories*—which relate the life of an Australian woman in the 1930s, '40s, and '50s—were told to me by my second cousin, Thomas Kelly the Fourth. If you like the story presented here, you can find more of them on my website.

Best regards, Pat.

https://www.patrickkellystories.com/

Fresh Faces and Crisp Uniforms

IN OCTOBER 1939, Sheila ambled onto the balcony of her suite at the Surfers Paradise Hotel. A slight breeze billowed the sheer curtains. The surf crashed nearby. A sandy track below her wound through palm trees to the beach. Although she'd checked in two weeks earlier, the salt air still thrilled her.

It had taken a couple hours the first day for her to recall how to surf. Unused muscles grew sore, but after the first week, it was like she'd never left the beach. The sheep farm might have been a thousand miles away—the rolling hills, the work, Tom and his family. The hundreds of details that had crowded her mind for years flew away like migrating birds. Only the ocean, the wind, and the mystery of Colin's intentions remained.

She could hardly stand still. Her weight shifted from one foot to the other and back again. She walked to the bureau and read Colin's telegram for the fourth time.

WILL ARRIVE BRISBANE MAIN STATION 17 OCTOBER 2 PM STOP CAN'T WAIT TO SEE YOU STOP

They had been apart for a full month. Before boarding the northbound train in Toowoomba, he had kissed her hard to make it last. By the time he returned, she would already be on holiday.

"I'll see you at Surfers Paradise," he had said.

"No," she had replied. "I'll meet you in Brisbane at the train station."

"Fair enough."

The sun had risen an hour earlier. She had four hours to kill before catching the bus to Brisbane. She'd go batty waiting in her room, so she hurried to dress in a bathing suit, loose-fitting pants, and a shirt. Downstairs, the bellman fetched her surfboard, and she hiked a few hundred feet to the beach.

Two surfers straddled their boards at the wave break, waiting for the perfect ride. She'd met them the first day. They worked in Brisbane during the week and camped nearby on the weekends to spend their days surfing. They were both eighteen, little more than boys. Few women surfed at the beach, so she had become an instant celebrity.

One of them caught a wave and rode it well. His name was Ned, and he finished his ride a few feet from her.

"Well, I'll be," he said, standing, "at last she arrives, the queen of Surfers Paradise. Did you sleep well, your highness?"

"Much better than you did in your tent, I'm sure." She walked in until the water reached her waist, then she hopped onto the board. "How are the waves?"

"A bit slow. I think they were waiting for you."

Ned paddled next to her. Ringlets of wet hair dangled in front of his face. "The best waves always wait for you."

"It has little to do with the quality of the wave and everything to do with the talent of the surfer."

He laughed and shook his head, and they paddled to the surf break.

The waves were quite good. She occupied her mind with the challenge of positioning the board, catching the waves, and moving her feet to control the ride.

She surfed for ninety minutes, returned to the hotel, dressed, had breakfast, and arranged a ride to the bus station. The bus was almost full, and she sat next to a middle-aged woman in a blue dress and a white hat.

"I like your hat," said Sheila, "very pretty."

"Thank you. I'm staying with my sister in town for the evening. We're going to a show. What about you?"

"Meeting my guy for a few days."

"Good for you. Is he joining the service?"

The woman referred to the Australian Imperial Force.

For nearly two decades, Australia had had little use for an army, but in reaction to global events, Prime Minister Menzies had announced the formation of the Second Australian Imperial Force.

"No," she said. "He's older."

Colin was thirty, further along in life than typical soldiers, who were often in their late teens or early twenties.

She could read the woman's mind. An older boyfriend? The woman glanced at Sheila's hands, perhaps searching for an engagement ring.

"Have you known each other a long time?"

"Two years."

"Oh, how nice."

Sheila's face grew warm.

The woman batted her eyes and pressed her lips together as if afraid she might actually speak her mind. Two years was a long time for a young couple to go without marrying. Some considered it odd.

Ignore her, Sheila reminded herself. Bigger issues were at stake than the prudish prejudices of a middle-aged biddy.

The global landscape had changed in a flash. After years of rising tensions and hopes for diplomacy, Germany had invaded Poland, which had driven Great Britain, France, Canada, and Australia (but not the US) to declare war on Germany.

And then there was Japan. The newspapers speculated that Japan—which had already occupied parts of China for eight years—now had designs on the rest of Asia.

The war had mobilized the entire country. Young men who volunteered traveled to new towns to join their units. When on break from their training, the young men went into town and met young women. The newspaper covered the story of a couple that had married two weeks after they met.

Which was outright lunacy. No matter how passionate the love, how could anyone decide to live with another person forever after only two weeks?

Yes, others were crazy, but not Sheila. She knew Colin well. She loved his laugh and the way he moved and how he made decisions.

Her stomach fluttered, and she tried but failed to pay attention to the passing scenery. The engine revved when the driver shifted gears. Her heart revved as well, for she suspected Colin would propose in the next few days.

Back in the Western Downs, she had found the perfect spot for a house, a flat piece of land nestled in trees at the top of a beautiful valley. She preferred the sea, but Colin's heart would always remain in the countryside. So be it. They could own their farms west of Toowoomba and take holidays at the coast.

In two hours, the bus entered the outskirts of Brisbane, which resembled the suburbs of Sydney. The big lawns and gardens gradually gave way to paved streets and telephone poles.

The streets grew wider and the buildings taller. Soldiers no older than her surfing buddies strolled on the sidewalks. They had fresh faces and wore crisp uniforms. They ventured about the city looking for action, strong and confident, as if they might believe themselves immortal.

The woman cocked an eyebrow and looked down. Sheila's knees bounced nonstop. She pressed her hands to her thighs to still them and smiled sweetly.

"I'm excited to see Colin."

"Naturally."

On the five-block walk from the bus depot, she tried to settle down. It seemed like forever since she'd seen him. She paced the platform until his train pulled into the station. So many cars and not a sign of him—had he missed it? Her heart skipped a beat.

Oh! There! He hung out the window of the next to the last car, his arms waving. She jumped and ran, reaching high to touch his fingers. He exited holding a suitcase. She kissed him madly, and he grabbed her and twirled her on the platform, oblivious of other passengers.

* * *

THEY SPENT TWO DAYS on the beach at Surfers Paradise. She tried to teach him to surf, but he didn't care much for it. He had always lived inland and wasn't a great swimmer. Instead, they went for walks on the beach and sat on towels in the afternoon. They talked about the cattle station, Colin's work, and the war.

At night, they ate in the fabulous dining room of the hotel. They had lobster the first night and steak the next. After dinner, they danced in the ballroom to big band tunes. They had become quite good at dancing, and she felt wonderful in his arms.

On the third night, he wore a new jacket and tie and ordered champagne. While they waited for the wine, he kept fidgeting, straightening his tie and running his hand through his hair. What was his problem? He was never nervous.

Oh, my goodness. He's going to propose.

Her heart pounded. Her throat grew thick. She moved her tableware farther apart, then closer together.

His eyes flitted around the dining room, stopped on her for a moment, and then darted to the stage.

"I need to tell you something," he said.

"Did you mean 'ask me something'?" she said.

Their eyes met. He searched hers as if trying to read her mind. Then he understood, and his face dropped.

Oh. He wasn't going to propose. She had misread him. She wanted to run from the table, to hide in her room, but she never ran from trouble.

"Sorry," he said. "I didn't mean . . . I'm not going to ask you to marry."

"Why not?" she said. "Don't you love me?"

"Yes. More than anything. I love you more than the land itself."

"Then what?"

"I've enlisted," he said.

"What?" she said.

Her mind raced. She saw an image of the uniformed boys sauntering on the sidewalks. They would travel far from Australia. But Colin was older; he was a stock and station agent. Farmers relied on him.

"The Eighteenth Brigade," he said.

"What?"

"The army will raise the Ninth Battalion here in Queensland."

All these numbers—the Eighteenth Brigade, the Ninth Battalion—they had nothing to do with Colin and her.

"The war has only begun," he said. "It will be much bigger than most people think. The Germans and Japanese have huge armies and great warships and guns. The world is going to war, and I have to do my bit."

"But you're needed here."

He shook his head. "The cattle will graze without me, and the sheep will be shorn without me."

"The armies can fight without you. Other men can die. Not you."

Many people thought of war as an adventure. Boys would become men; they would amass great triumphs and return home with great tales, or so they thought. But she had studied the First World War. Thousands of Australians never came back.

"We could still marry," she said. "We could marry tomorrow."

He shook his head. "I'll never understand how couples can marry the week before the man leaves for training camp. It makes no sense."

She could have tried to change his mind, pestered him with arguments for an hour or more, but he'd made his decision. He had reflected on the pros and cons, and settled on his course.

"Will you wait for me?" he asked.

"Of course," she said. "For as long as it takes. When will you leave?"

The skin around his eyes grew tight.

"Soon," she said.

Her chest fell. He'd be gone for months, perhaps a year. Tears threatened to fall, but she wiped them away. Crying would serve no purpose now.

The waiter brought the bottle and filled their glasses.

"Well," she said. "Let's not mope about it. We have champagne to drink."

* * *

THEY SPENT ANOTHER week at Surfers Paradise. More dancing. Walks on the beach. Afternoons in the late sunshine. And then they rode the bus to the city, and he kissed her goodbye.

Two days later, on the train back to Toowoomba, a light rain fell on the sheep farms she passed. The cloud cover deepened the green of the paddocks. She blinked hard and sniffled. The sheep huddled against the chill. They looked sad, as if they knew their stock and station agent had wandered off to war.

End of Excerpt from *The Sheila Stories*

As of May 2019, *The Sheila Stories* are unpublished. But you can find them on my website. Best, Pat.

patrickkellystories.com

ACKNOWLEDGMENTS

THANK YOU TO READERS who recommend my work to their friends and submit honest reviews to Amazon. In this game, word of mouth is everything.

I traveled to Santorini on holiday in 2010. The view of the caldera from the top of the cliff in Imerovigli stunned me with its beauty, much like Joe Robbins was transfixed when Petros first delivered him to the Liakáda Suites. I wrote the first draft of this novel soon after returning home. It took nine years and three other Joe Robbins novels for me to finally finish *The Island Thief.* I hope the good citizens of Santorini will forgive me for falsely portraying the island as being subject to a level of corruption. As far as I know, this is not true. The towns depicted in the novel are real, but the characters, hotels, restaurants, bars, and events are fictitious.

Germancreative designed the book cover. Liz Ferry of Per Se Editing edited the manuscript.

ABOUT THE AUTHOR

I WAS BORN in Yorktown, Virginia, (site of the decisive battle of the Revolutionary War) and received an engineering degree from the University of Virginia and an M.B.A. from Carnegie-Mellon University.

After school, I moved to Dallas, Texas, to work in finance at American Airlines and went on to become the chief financial officer for a number of high-tech companies, including Sabre, Trilogy, Vignette, and Workfront. At one point, we sold a company I worked for, and since then I've split my time between working as a freelance CFO and writing.

I love writing crime thrillers. They are the kind of books I like to read—chock-full of suspense, bursting with action, and topped off with a trace of romance.

Please leave an honest rating and review of this novel on Amazon. It will only take you a few minutes and will help me sell more books.

KEEP IN TOUCH

Website: www.patrickkellystories.com
Facebook: www.facebook.com/patrickkellywriter

Subscribe to the PK Monthly on my website to get a free download of the Joe Robbins short story *The Ringer,* which is not available anywhere else. Each month, I'll send you a brief note with links to unpublished works and other good stuff.

Made in the USA
Columbia, SC
28 April 2019